a Belladonna Ink novel

# Far From Home

## Lorelie Brown

**RIPTIDE**
PUBLISHING

Riptide Publishing
PO Box 1537
Burnsville, NC 28714
www.riptidepublishing.com

Far From Home
Copyright © 2016 by Lorelie Brown

Cover art: L.C. Chase, lcchase.com/design.htm
Editors: Sarah Lyons and Gwen Hayes
Layout: L.C. Chase, lcchase.com/design.htm

ISBN: 978-1-62649-452-7

First edition
August, 2016

Also available in ebook:
ISBN: 978-1-62649-451-0

a Belladonna Ink novel

# Far From Home

## Lorelie Brown

RIPTIDE
PUBLISHING

*For the people who love me. I'm consistently amazed to find there are so many.*

table of

# Contents

# chapter

One

"*I* would marry you," I say.

Naturally, the entire party goes silent.

The bottom drops out of my stomach. What used to be pleasant, cooling condensation on my glass suddenly becomes lube-levels of slickness. I could drop my wine at any moment.

Worst of all, Pari Sadashiv is looking at me. In the small group of four people standing around the useless fireplace of an acquaintance's apartment, Pari's green eyes are the only ones that matter.

"Don't be ridiculous, Rachel," Krissy says with a laugh. "No one would believe you. You'd have INS on you in an instant."

I manage to smile a little bit when Krissy and her friend Chase laugh. Pari doesn't look away from me though.

"It's not INS anymore, since the Department of Homeland Security took over. But why is it so unbelievable?" Pari's mouth tips into a tiny smile. "I'll have you know my *amma* would be happy if I married anyone at this point. She doesn't even know I want to give up my H-1B visa just to be independently employed. If she knew that, she'd find the first breathing person who'd marry me."

Krissy grins. "It's Rachel. She's not gay."

"Weren't you dating that one guy? Who ran that club?" Chase helpfully offers.

My cheeks are flaming hot. Krissy is talking about me as if I'm not even here. Or as if I'm a child. Not like Krissy would allow children in her ultramodern apartment. They might try to color the begging-for-it matte gray walls.

Why am I here, for that matter? It's not as if I'm actually friends with Krissy. We went to film school together, though she had her daddy's money funding her. The tiny production company I work with is too precarious to risk upsetting one of Hollywood's inheriting golden girls, though. Showing up to her birthday party is mandatory if I don't want to feel a knife in my back sometime in the next year. She's that sort of girl.

"She could be bisexual," Pari says calmly. "They aren't required to wear signs any longer."

I narrow my eyes. Had she just subtly compared our host to a Nazi? Not that it's undeserved, but Krissy's usual guests aren't often so willing to throw shade.

Krissy giggles. "That's so true. You know, I kissed a girl once. At a sorority party. I was sooooo drunk."

I turn my wineglass in my hands. "Was that the night the Jell-O shooters wouldn't set, so you bought a brand-new trash can and poured them all in together?"

"Wasn't college the best?" Krissy sighs.

Well, no. That isn't what I meant. More like how half our friends nearly gave themselves alcohol poisoning that night. Fifty grand in student debt well spent in order to learn to never mix alcohols. Lovely. Glad I tossed away my time on that.

It worked for Krissy, at least. After graduation she took a job as an assistant in her father's studio and has spent the last three years making money, working her way up rapidly to assistant director. I stupidly went on to grad school to tack another twenty grand on my debt, leaving me too skilled to be entry-level. Who's the smart one now?

I knock back the last of my red wine so I can say, "I'm going to get a refill." I wave my glass as I leave.

Maybe I'll live wildly and mix wines.

At least the kitchen is quiet. Krissy—or her catering company—set up a dizzying array of snacks and wine near the picture window in the living room. The sparkling lights of Los Angeles spread beneath the window as C-list stars compare casting call notes. No one wants to be so passé as to hang out in the kitchen. I like my wine cold, though.

To be honest, I like silence better, as well as not having to look at the orgy of food that's laid out. I open the glass-fronted fridge and snag the bottle of wine I've hidden for myself. I hope Krissy has a drawerful of takeout menus somewhere, or that she has the DoorDash app loaded on her front page, because otherwise I'll have to admit she lives on cucumber water and plain Greek yogurt. My jealousy probably isn't healthy.

"Thank you for saying you'd marry me."

I yelp and spin. Because I'm graceful like that. I try to clap my hand to my chest, but cold wine splashes over my knuckles instead. "Jesus."

"I'm sorry to startle you." Pari's standing in the doorway. Even though her dress looks like silk, she doesn't seem to mind that the flared skirt brushes against the doorjamb. Her dark brown hair spills around her shoulders, turning the dark-blue boatneck into a bejeweled setting.

I shrug. "Awkward is my personal brand. I probably shouldn't have said that. About marrying you. I'm sorry if it was weird."

"It wasn't weird. I promise." Pari tips her head enough that long hair slides over her shoulder. "I'm the one who was crass enough to talk about my visa difficulties."

I love her voice. It isn't only the lilting cadence of her native India mixed with crisp Britishness, it's the sweet kindness that is absolutely letting me off the hook.

I lift the wine bottle I'm still holding, only to realize there's some on my fingers. I transfer the bottle to my other hand and lick my knuckles. "Would you like some? I'll let you pour so I don't make any more of an ass of myself."

"I'll take some, but not for that reason." Her charm flashes as she moves, like she carries a bubble of rarified air.

As Pari stands next to me at the slate counter and reaches for one of the hanging glasses above us, my breath catches. Pari has the elegance that I have always lacked and always admired.

"So are you bisexual?" Even the question that would have been unbelievably rude from someone else seems mildly curious from her gentle tone.

"Oh! Um, no. Sorry?" My heartbeat drowns all my other senses out.

"You certainly don't have to apologize for that. Though I have to admit I'm a little disappointed."

The tips of my ears tingle, and my stomach takes a funny swoop. "Disappointed? Why?"

Pari glances sideways at me. Her throat is long and lovely. "I'm sorry if this is forward, but Krissy said you have large bills and a job that doesn't keep up."

"They're student loans." The swoop of my stomach turns into the hot coals of embarrassment that Krissy has implied I've been recklessly spending. "I have a master's. I didn't have any family to help."

"A master's," Pari echoes. She nods. "A master's is excellent."

"Not when it's an MFA in film. Even with a job, I can't afford to make my minimum payments." I try to make my smile wry, but based on how awkward I feel, it's probably somewhere on the pitiful spectrum.

"Which makes me wonder if we could come to a mutual understanding after all."

It's my turn to echo Pari. "Mutual understanding?"

"You see, I'm not rich per se," Pari says as if those words make perfect sense in that combination. "But I'm comfortable. I wouldn't be considering entering consulting and giving up my work visa if I didn't have a cushion."

"Uh-huh." I nod as if I have even a slight hint where this is heading.

"And I *am* a lesbian." Pari turns and leans a hip against the counter. "A gold-star lesbian, as a matter of fact."

"Congratulations?"

"It works for me." Her pale-green eyes glow with amusement. Especially against the rich, clear brown of her skin, they're magical. "No one would be surprised if I marry a woman."

"I'm not sure what you're . . ." Except I do know. I have an idea I know exactly where this is going in that split-second way where I could shut it all down or maybe change the entire course of my life with one conversation.

It's happened once before, when I admitted to my friend Nikki soon after graduation that I had a problem. A problem with a big old capital P, a life-changing Problem. That had been the right choice too. I'm not one to shy away from change.

I hold up a hand. "No. Wait, that is . . . Will you marry me, Pari?"

"Why don't we start with a first date? A chance to talk about it in depth?" She grins, suddenly more minxish than elegant. "After all, if we get married, we'll need to get our stories straight. And we really ought to find out if we can be friends at least."

Pari has the most beautiful smile. Her teeth are perfectly straight and even. I'm dazzled.

I lift my glass in a toast. "To first dates that aren't first dates."

"And to the American immigration process."

# Two

My hands start shaking the moment I ring the doorbell of Pari's condo even though I was fine until now. I immediately shove them in the pockets of my hoodie. She answers the door quickly, as if she's been hovering and waiting.

She looks great. And I am severely underdressed. I've worn shorts and a shirt from H&M under the hoodie, with my hair in a ponytail. Pari is wearing another of those stunning dresses. I'm glad we're eating in her apartment or I'd be even more self-conscious.

"Nice building," I manage.

"Thank you. Would you like to come in?" She has killer heels on, in a light brown that's nude on her and makes her legs look like they go on for miles.

"I don't live super far away. On the other side of San Sebastian. The side that's farther away from the ocean." I think I'm babbling. Of course I am. "I bet you have a hell of a view."

"It's not bad. Come this way."

Pari leads me to the right, into the living room. A wide expanse of blue is the decorating focus.

"'Not bad'? Okay, so you speak in understatements. Got that, at least." The view is mind-blowing. I've always loved the ocean, and seeing that just-right blue makes me breathe a little easier. Makes my shoulders loosen up.

"To be fair, I saw much better when I was house hunting. They were directly on the sand, not across a road."

"Yeah, but that's not just any old road. That's the Pacific Coast Highway. It's part of the view itself. History is on that road."

Pari looks back out the window as if she's seeing the gray bottom border and the zooming cars in a whole new way. The condo is too high up to hear more than an occasional buzz, so the noise isn't too much. The balcony is long and narrow.

"Did you grow up around here?" Pari asks.

I nod. This is supposed to be about finding compatibility. I can do that. "Born and raised. I graduated from San Sebastian high school, and then I stayed nearby for college."

"UC Irvine?"

I'm not surprised she'd guess that. UCI is a respectable branch of the University of California system, but certain ones have more cachet than others. "A little farther than that, but not much. Just UCLA."

"Why do you downplay it like that? UCLA is a fantastic school."

"I was dumb enough to get a film degree without having the passion needed to claw my way up in Hollywood." I drag my gaze away from the ocean and give her a sidelong glance. "And then I followed it up with an MFA from USC. Because the only thing better than a useless degree is a useless degree that costs a hell of a lot of money." I emphasize my self-depreciation with a flashy spread of my hands.

Pari looks at me for a moment. She's unreadable, but I don't know if it's because I'm not on her level or because she's closed off. "Would you like something to drink? I have tea, wine, or water."

It would probably be strange if I ask for water. "Tea sounds nice."

Pari leads the way to the kitchen, and I try not to be too obvious as I crane my neck to take everything in. The condo isn't huge, but it's roomy enough. Without seeing the bedrooms, I can't pinpoint a square footage, but it's certainly more than enough space for one woman. Maybe even two if the second is careful and self-contained.

The kitchen is lovely. Cast iron and copper and silver pots hang from a rack above the island, which is topped with natural-stained wood. They obviously were chosen for use instead of appearance, but that doesn't keep them from being beautiful. "Do you cook a lot, or is this for show?"

"Somewhere in between. I do love to cook, but I don't often have time."

"I love to eat. This could be a good thing." Or terrible. Because while I do love to eat, I don't exactly have a healthy relationship with food.

Pari pings on that immediately. Her glance skims over me from my head to my oversized hoodie to my toes. "You don't look like you like to eat. No, I shouldn't have said that. That was rude." I pull my mouth up into a smile, but it doesn't feel the least bit happy. "So I don't usually mention this the second time I meet someone, but I'm a recovering anorexic."

"I'm so sorry for what I said." Her cheeks turn ruddy. Her fingertips rise to her collarbones. "I'm . . . Oh. Wow. I'm really, really sorry. I didn't use wheat, because it seems like everyone is avoiding it, but I didn't ask about anything else."

It's kind of adorable that I can shake her at all. Maybe I'll be able to remember this rather than the burn of her accidental stinger. I rub her shoulder. "It's okay. I'm in recovery. There's lots of stuff I eat. That's the point."

Pari touches her temple. "Now I've caused you to reassure *me*. I'm sorry. Again."

"And it's okay. Again." A real smile takes over me. "Though this *is* kind of why I don't tell people this quickly. Normally."

"I can see why."

Pari fusses over serving the meal. She takes a copper dish from the oven and sets it on a trivet. When she opens the lid and the warm, rich scent of potatoes wafts toward me, I try to distract myself. The handle is printed with the name Mauviel and the year 1830. She buys her pots from a company that's been around that long? I wonder how many years T-fal has racked up.

The main meal is summer vegetables layered in a beautiful spiral and baked. Once we're seated across from each other, I serve myself a modest portion.

"I tried not to cook with most of the major allergens, but if you want me to be careful of anything else, just let me know."

"No allergies." I cut my food into bite-sized pieces, though not as small as I would like. I allow myself small indulgences in my disorder. Sometimes. Only when I'm really unnerved. I set both knife and fork down between bites so I can better enjoy every mouthwatering taste. "You're an amazing cook."

"Thank you."

I think about asking why she didn't make Indian food but almost instantly decide that's silly. Why wouldn't she make delicious French food if she's capable? We fill the air with a few minutes of small talk on how dry the weather has been and how desperately our state needs rain. Not exactly the most compelling conversation, but okay. I could hang with her company for a while.

Toward the end of the meal, Pari sets her silverware down and folds her hands in her lap. "May I ask you something?"

"Sure." I lean my elbows on the arms of my chair. My choppy ponytail brushes across the back of my neck.

"Why did you get your degree in film if you say you're lacking ambition?"

"The short answer? Because I wasn't always completely aimless. The long answer has to do with my eating disorder. I became disillusioned with the industry. Which I guess is still the short version of the long answer."

"Fair point." She fiddles with the metal handle of her spoon. "I don't have enough money to make your student debt go away. I wish I could offer that."

"You wish it because you'd like to start a side job as a fairy godmother, or you wish it so I'd be more likely to agree?"

I like making Pari laugh. "Is it terrible if I say both?"

"Not terrible. Just honest, and honesty seems like something we need if we're gonna do this."

"Are we?" She leans toward me. Excitement lights her up.

"I don't know yet," I say. I like being in control of her excitement. It's exhilarating. "Tell me why."

"Why I want this, or why *you* should agree?"

I shrug. I push my plate toward the center of the table and lean my elbows on the edge of the jacquard tablecloth. The floral pattern is saved from boredom by a red border. "Either. Both."

"I've been in California on an H-1B visa for several years. I work in personnel logistics management, enabling companies to execute multistructured tasks with efficient automation—and I did notice your eyes glaze over there."

I jump. "Did not."

"Honesty . . ."

"Okay. I may have faded out."

"I don't blame you. Few people find my field even tolerably exciting."

"But it is to you."

"You don't have to sound *so* doubtful. I like being able to create a viable, tangible change in a workplace's office culture and efficacy."

"But you don't want to do that at your current job anymore?"

"I want to go wider." Pari spreads her hands. It's like she can see some interwoven web of businesses between her fingers. "I'm ready to go into consulting. My visa is sponsored by my employer. The two are not compatible."

"What kind of commitment am I looking at here?"

She balks, leaning away from me for a moment. Her gaze flicks toward the kitchen, then back again. Abashed? "At least two years. After two years of marriage, I can apply for my green card. There are interviews required, and we'll have to provide evidence of the legitimacy of our marriage. If this arrangement is still suiting both of us, it might be helpful if we could continue long enough for me to apply for citizenship, but if I need to, I can live on my green card."

"That's the permanent resident thing?" I've done a tiny bit of googling. Though I've probably done more daydreaming about what my life could be like if I had even a little help with my student loans.

"Yes. It really can be permanent. But if we document our so-called relationship well enough, maybe visit a counselor on the way out, I could conceivably apply for citizenship even after we've divorced."

I could be a divorced woman. How strange. I haven't ever thought of myself in the role. Doesn't seem terrible to me though. "Isn't there an easier way out? No other kinds of visa?"

"Immigration has tightened the requirements for self-employment. There are other possibilities, but not as easy as marriage."

"Two years of marriage doesn't seem that easy to me. Not if we're talking about my parents' example."

"Were they not happy?"

"Pretty much no. They managed to tolerate each other until I moved out of the house for college. Then they divorced. Six months later, my dad died of a heart attack. My mom seemed . . . relieved more than anything."

"Is she around?"

"She moved to Alaska." I shrug, still as confused and abandoned as ever over that one. I've learned to accept it, but I'll never learn to understand it.

"My parents are very happy." Pari smiles as if she's remembering something very sweet about them. "Their marriage was arranged. My mother is still confident in her ability to find me a nice doctor within a week if I breathe a word to her."

"You don't want to take that option?"

"Still that gay thing. I've been out to them for a number of years, and they've come around, but not so much that *amma* will matchmake me with a woman if she can help it. And I'm out enough in my professional world that it will raise alarms if I were to suddenly marry a man."

"Is that why you want to stay?" My cheeks turn simmering hot. I'm probably bright pink. "God. Listen to me. I sound like I'm interrogating you."

"It seems mutual. You told me something personal as well."

"And I'll answer more too."

Pari has earnest eyes, her positive intentions smoothing the wrinkles from her brow. Her nose is softly rounded at the end and paired with lips that are generously curved as well. "Yes. Being gay is a large part of why I don't want to go back. Plus I simply like America. I have a good life here."

"Why don't you have a girlfriend? Someone to marry for real?"

"I had a long-term relationship. We broke up." Her eyes go cool, and she backs her chair up from the table as if to put distance between us. "Would you like to see the rest of the condo? It's home."

"Sure." I push up from my chair and start gathering my dishes. "Just tell me where to put these?"

Pari tries to demur but I won't accept a no. I didn't manage to finish my food with all our talking, and I don't want to put her through the trouble of scraping food into the trash. She might think it's a reflection on her cooking when it absolutely isn't. I even rinse my plate before putting it in the stainless-steel-fronted dishwasher. I have to admit that I want to establish myself as a potentially conscientious roommate too.

"I'll be honest," Pari says, "when I said 'show you the apartment,' I mostly meant the second bedroom. You've seen everything else."

Except I haven't seen Pari's bedroom. It feels too intimate to ask, like I'd be inviting myself into her truest, deepest life.

"So you'd want me to move in here?"

"Unless you object? I own it—well, the bank and I do. I could conceivably rent it out and move in with you."

I can't help but laugh. "I live in a studio apartment. That doesn't seem like a good idea."

"Then I would love to offer you this room." She pushes the door open. "As you can see, it's currently my office, but the master bedroom is large enough that I'll be able to put my desk in there."

"And I'd get that view?"

A sliding glass door leads out onto the same balcony that's accessible from the living room.

"If you want it."

"Rent?"

"Free. No utilities either. I already cover it all by myself now. This could take over two years from marriage to green card. Longer if we agree to take me to full citizenship. I can't afford to pay for your loans outright, but I can help occasionally. And I can do this. I don't know how much you're spending on rent now—"

"As much as my base loan payment." And man, is that so damn painful every month. I can't remember the last time I got to have dinner out. Sushi is a wet dream for me. I shove a hand out to shake. "Consider me in."

"But the details?"

"We can work them out later. We're going to have plenty of time. You and I are getting married."

"*I*t's amazing what lengths you'll go to for a nice apartment in this market."

I stop with both hands on the flaps of a moving box and look up at Nikki. My best friend since forever—or middle school, sometimes it's hard to tell the difference—stands in the open sliding glass door, her face turned toward the sun. Her long ponytail hangs down her back, perfectly still except for a few strands being tossed in the breeze. She's like me, born and raised in San Sebastian, and as a result, she's a sun worshipper of the very highest order.

"Was that supposed to sound so bitter? I didn't think you, of all people, would object to a gay marriage. Or to improvements in my life."

Nikki wrinkles her nose. "I'm pretty sure Skylar isn't the marrying type. I think it's in the 'I'm a hard-ass tattoo artist' creed."

"Don't tell me there's trouble in paradise." I lean back on my butt. Nikki keeps her problems close and her happiness closer. It only makes me more willing than ever to drop anything and listen if she's actually going to ask for help.

But she waves a hand. "Not anything worth worrying about."

I'm not sure about that. The last two times Nikki has been home from the pro-surfing competition circuit, she's seemed a little less happy. But if she isn't going to talk about it, I'm not going to pry.

I know what keeping a secret is like.

"I thought you were here to help me move in, not judge me for my life choices?"

"I helped haul your boxes up here. Where you put everything is up to you. You're the one who's going to be living in this room for two years."

"I have the rest of the place."

"Do you?" Nikki crosses her arms. "Like, I know you can go watch TV in the living room, but can you paint the walls if you want to?"

"I have no idea." I push up from the floor and make a production of brushing off the butt of my shorts. Mostly so I don't have to look at her. "But you know what I *can* do?"

"What?"

"Take that hundred bucks that I would have spent on paint and send it to Fannie Mae. So maybe I have half a chance of digging out from under my debt before it's time to freak out about retirement instead. Even if this doesn't work out? Even if it crashes and burns and I'm scrambling for an annulment in three months? That's three less months of loan payments."

"Fewer."

"What?"

"Three fewer months."

I ball up a shirt from the box at my feet and chuck it at her. She bats it away, making the experience wholly unfulfilling. "Oh, shut up already."

I don't think this will go pear-shaped in three months. I think it's going to work. There's something I like about Pari. She seems so cool and collected, but then she'll look at me with those eyes that reveal a wellspring of compassion. I feel safe around her. I know she didn't mean it when she said I don't look like I eat.

"Let's go christen the beach," Nikki says.

"Don't say it like that. It sounds dirty."

"Oh, sweetie." Nikki smiles and tilts her head angelically while she folds her hands as if in prayer. "Does it hurt your virgin ears? Besides, you know if that were what I meant, I'd have just said it."

"My ears are not virgin."

"I think you regrew. You haven't been done right in forever."

"That's probably a good thing." I made lots of mistakes when I wasn't well. When I was sickest with my problems. Nikki and I once bonded over our poor vaginal choices. But she reformed by finding true love, and I reformed by gluing my parts shut.

Nikki and I change into our swimsuits, but hit a snag when I can only find one beach towel. "Damn it, I thought I'd put them all in this box."

Nikki flicks the one towel. "It would seem like you didn't."

"Whatever. I'm going to see if Pari has any."

I find her at the dining room table with a salad, a spreadsheet, and an open laptop. A narrow furrow connects her dark brows as she stares at the glowing screen. The salad next to her is only half-eaten, but she's tapping her blunt fingernails on the slate-topped table instead of holding her fork.

I stop in the archway. "Everything okay?"

"Hmm?" She blinks as if shaking out cobwebs. "Sure. Just trying to puzzle through a problem."

"On a Saturday?"

"Once my consultancy gets fired up, my hours will become incredibly irregular. Saturdays will mean nothing to me."

"Then you should take advantage of them while they're still a possibility. Wanna come down to the beach with Nikki and me?" We'd spent four hours together as we all loaded and unloaded boxes. It wouldn't be awkward to unwind. I'm still surprised to hear the invitation coming out of my own mouth. I shouldn't be though. We're going to be together for the next two years. A friendship is the bare minimum we need.

Pari is going to refuse. I'm not sure how I know, because it isn't as if I actually *know* her yet. But it's there in the shape of her face, in the way her lush mouth is suddenly . . . not lush. "I have to get this worked out. I don't know when I'll be able to cut ties and open my consultancy. I can't afford to leave any big projects in the lurch."

I wish she looked just a little bit more regretful, but I make myself shrug. "Maybe next time. Do you have a beach towel we can use? I can only find one."

"Of course. They're in the linen closet at the end of the hall next to the bathroom. Beach towels are on the bottom shelf. Feel free to use anything in there."

I wouldn't though. I know myself. I would ask her each and every step of the way, to make sure I'm not overstepping anything.

Weird way to start a marriage, but I'd probably do the same thing in a regular dating situation.

Nikki and I stop by the storage locker at the garage level and pick up two of my boards. Pari doesn't have much in there, so I was able to just kind of shove my whole rack in without thinking about it. Now I take a moment to look around. I touch the seat of a cruiser-style bicycle leaning against the chain-link wall.

"She doesn't seem very outdoorsy."

Nikki lifts a brow. She scoops one of my fish surfboards off the rack and tucks it under one arm. "You'd know that already if it weren't for the fast-forward style of all this."

I sigh. The small of my back hurts. My therapist says that's where I carry all my tension, but I know that isn't right. I carry it all in my stomach and my chest, because they are always knotted tight. I cross my arms and rub my collarbone. "Look, I think we need to get something out in the open. I'm doing this. I'm going to marry her, and if you continue with the negative comments, I don't know how I'll be able to handle that."

Nikki's eyes go wide. She leans the fish back against the line of surfboards, and even though she's being careful to not hurt my gear, she's moving quickly. The need to make me feel better flows from her. She wraps both hands around my upper arms and gives them a quick rub.

"Sure, sure. I'm sorry. I'll stop." Her mouth twists into a wry smile. "It's just been kind of a rapid adjustment."

"I took a risk by telling you that this isn't some romance. You're the only person I *plan* to tell about the arrangement, and I did it because I'll need a safe space. Someone to talk to."

"I will be there. Here. I promise." She gives me a decisive nod. That's the thing about Nikki—sometimes she can be a little obtuse, but if I ever manage to articulate that I need her, she's willing to dump her heart out on my toes. Or go to battle for me. The best sort of friend.

We each pick boards, but once we get out to the beach, I'm not exactly rushing to hit the waves. I flick my towel out and sit on it. With my wrists draped on my knees, I take a deep breath and try to connect to the rest of me. My toes are on the hot sand. More warmth comes through the towel under my butt.

"I'm going to head out," Nikki says.

I flap a hand at her and let myself fall back. The sun attacks me from the front and the sand comforts me from beneath. Living right here at the edge of the ocean is such a plus in this situation.

When stress gets to me, I'll be able to come out here. My old apartment wasn't too many actual miles from the water, but the traffic meant it took a half hour to get myself hauled to the beach. That doesn't count finding parking.

Not a problem now. I've joined the elite.

Whatever that's going to mean for me.

I let my hands rest at my sides on the towel, with the tip of my thumbs barely grazing my hips. I don't like touching myself. I don't like the texture of my skin or the softness beneath.

Which means the second the thought crosses my mind, I force myself to touch my thighs. I lay my palms flat on top of them. I've already been heated by the sun, and my palms are slightly damp. They come together unwillingly, but this is my own flesh. I should be used to it. By now, at least. My therapist will be so disappointed in me.

When a shadow crosses over me, I'm almost relieved. I crack one eye open and squint up. At first I don't know who it is because their face is cast in deep shadow. Then I do.

It's Pari.

"Hi!" I lean up on an elbow and shield my eyes with a hand at my brow. "You decided to come down?"

Well duh. Obviously she has. What I actually mean is I hadn't expected it, but I can't seem to make those words come out. Naturally. I pray she doesn't notice my awkwardness or, if she does, that maybe she'll think it's part of my normal personality. It is, to an extent, but it seems to go into overdrive around her.

"I decided you were right. If I'm going to lose my Saturdays, I should take advantage of them now." Pari lays out her towel and gracefully sits cross-legged on it. She's wearing a bright-red bikini with retro styling. The bottoms are full enough to come to her belly button, but she still has a softness to her tummy that I would absolutely despise on myself. On her it makes sense, because it's balanced by the gentle swells of her hips and by her breasts. Because, good Lord, what a rack she has. The heart-shaped neckline of the bikini top plumps them into mounds anyone would envy.

My hands sneak over my stomach, and I smash inward just a little. Maybe if I had breasts like those, I wouldn't mind roundness on me everywhere else. I don't mind it at all on Pari. She's richly shaped. Whatever force made her used a wealth of materials and never stinted.

I feel small and spare next to her. Slight. I look up at the sky, at the plain-blue expanse that's a Southern California day, but I can't help sneaking glances at her again.

"You surf?" she eventually asks, breaking the silence that squirms between us.

"Mm-hmm." I push up on my elbows again. The posture scoops my stomach out to look hollow, and I want to pretend I don't notice, but I do. What I can't tell is if I want Pari to notice too. "Since middle school."

"Who taught you?"

I point out at the water, where Nikki is bobbing in the limp surf, waiting for waves that don't seem to be coming. "Nikki's brother is five years older than her. He surfed and we kept stealing his boards. At first we were dragging them all the way to the beach just to look cool—how dumb is that?—but then we decided we wanted to learn. So we took turns. We kinda taught each other."

"Your dedication is admirable."

I giggle. Then I clap my hand over my mouth. I'm probably blushing, because seriously? A giggle? Talk about an inappropriate response. "There's nothing about dedication. I'm a half-assed surfer at best. Nikki competes."

"But you've not neglected it."

"I'd be out there right now if I were serious." I splay myself flat on the sand and briefly close my eyes. "Instead of thinking about a nap."

"I don't have anything I do now that I did in high school."

"I bet that's not true."

"Sometimes it feels true. I live in a different country. I run now. I cook foods I had never heard of before moving here. All my habits are different." She grins widely enough that I can see the line of her gums above her teeth. Her smile is huge. "I'm even a lesbian here, and I'm not at home."

"Is India home still, though?"

"Always will be."

"Where? In particular, I mean."

"Tamil Nadu." She slants a look out of the corner of her eyes, as if she's waiting for something. I don't know what it is, which makes low-grade panic settle in my chest like a flapping, frantic bird. I probably should know where Tamil Nadu is, but I don't. Americanized worldview fail. I manage to creak out an encouraging nod so that she goes on. "It's in South India. On the eastern side. My mother is originally from New Delhi, but her father traveled for business and met my father's family. *Amma* moved south when she married my father. I'm lucky that her side of the family is progressive."

"I know you want to stay now, but did you want to come to the states? Or were you more reluctant?"

Her eyes go wide, and she gives me a half smile. Her hair slips over her rounded shoulder. I want to push it back into place.

"No one's ever asked me that before." She doesn't push her hair over her shoulder. She combs her fingers through the ends instead. On another woman, the gesture would have been flirtatious, but on Pari it seems much more simple. As if she's actually trying to make sure she has no snarls. "Everyone here seems to assume that of course I would wish to be here. They like their lives, after all, and everyone knows that India is a shithole."

She says it so matter-of-factly I almost miss it. "But you don't think that."

"India is a country, same as any other. It has its beautiful places and its less-than-pleasant places. Most of the people who assume that India is horrible also wouldn't go into Detroit on a bet. And no. I didn't want to come here."

"How old were you?"

"Twenty. I came for graduate school, to get my MBA."

"At twenty. Impressive."

She shrugged. "I worked hard."

I don't know what that's like, to acknowledge your gifts and capabilities in three little words. I've worked hard in my life too, but I'd choke if I tried to say it so simply. I envy her. I want to get closer to her, to find out if some of that assuredness could sink into me. Maybe by osmosis?

Maybe if I was her, I wouldn't have to be me.

"*I*'d like you to be with me when I tell my parents that we're getting married."

The words compute, but make absolutely no sense at the same time. I stop where I am, in the act of reaching for a water glass. "What?"

"On Skype."

"Oh. Well that makes a little more sense." I grab the glass and shut the white cabinet.

Everything is so shiny in her kitchen. Making cheesy toast seems almost inadequate, but it's what I want for lunch. Slice of bread, slice of cheddar. I have a pile of berries too. All together my lunch comes in around 250 calories. My nutritionist will want more protein included, so I'll probably grab an ounce of turkey jerky too. Maybe.

I'm such a good little patient that I only get checkups with the nutritionist every three months. This is a vast improvement on the weekly appointments I used to have. I see my therapist, Karen, more often.

Pari slides onto a barstool at the island beneath her beautiful copper pots. She drags a bowl of strawberries closer to her and starts nibbling. "Would you want to visit?"

"India?" I glance at her, then go back to watching my food in the toaster to make sure it hits exactly the right level of melted and bubbly without the edges of the toast getting a step past golden brown. I'm particular about my food. It's one of my problems. "Sure. I like traveling."

"Could you get the time off?"

"That's the benefit of being in a position like mine. I'm kind of nonvital. If I have the time between projects, or if I'm willing to take no pay, I can go anytime."

"I don't know that we will, but it might help with my mother to be able to offer a visit."

She's fidgeting with one of the strawberries, her nail digging into the stem under the leafy cap. Red juice drips onto the slate-gray top of the island. Her eyes are clouded.

I take my food out of the toaster oven and drop it on my plate. Before I can even think about it, I'm across the room and folding my hand over hers. Her skin is warm. She looks up at me, making the curtain of her hair slide. The heady scent of coconut finds me.

"It'll be okay," I say.

She looks at our hands stacked together, then up at me. "You're a very positive person, aren't you?"

I shake my head in automatic denial. That's the outside me, what I do for everyone else. They all deserve good things and to have faith in themselves. That's not the same thing as being positive. No one hears the way I talk to myself. I'd stop if I knew how.

"It's not a bad thing," Pari says, as if she's assumed my denial is something else. "To be openhearted . . ."

"Openhearted sounds much better than having my 'head in the clouds.'"

"Is that what's been said to you before?"

"A time or two." I carry my plate and bowl to the island and sit next to Pari. I rip my toast into four squares so that I know exactly what I'm eating. Each square will hopefully take me five bites. "My mom would have had it Sharpied under my degree. And ta-da! She was right, wasn't she?"

"Alaska doesn't seem too practical."

"She works for an oil company." I pull one of the toast quarters into two pieces. "Don't imagine her in a cabin somewhere being all backwoodsy. She's in as close to a penthouse as Anchorage has."

"Still, that seems like a lot of negativity to fight through on your graduation day." Pari's eyes sing their compassion in a face that's otherwise so composed.

"Oh, she didn't come to my graduation." The nibble of toast sticks at the back of my throat. I swallow it down with effort. "She had a conference that she couldn't get out of. She was the keynote speaker."

"I see." Two little words. It's Pari's turn to reach for me.

She touches my upper arm with only two fingertips at first. That's enough to let me breathe again. When her palm slides up my skin to cup my shoulder, I almost shudder. A soft summer rain of comfort washes over me. This is a different sort of touching than the stuff I get from Nikki or my other friends. The attention slut in me sucks it all up like the chrome off a truck hitch.

My friends are good to me, and they give me bottles of wine and shoulders to cry on when I'm upset, but that's not the same thing as having someone inside the bubble that is you. I spent so long encircling my bubble with chicken wire in order to hide my problems that sometimes I don't know how to take it down. Here, in this moment, I've let Pari inside.

I'm feeling better emotionally, but I let my head droop a little anyway so she won't take her hand away from my shoulder. She's not mindlessly patting or petting me. She's holding still. I'm holding still. That's the thing. We're still together.

Eventually, I can't help looking up from underneath the fall of my hair and giving her a little smile. I don't want to take advantage of her, make her give more than she feels comfortable giving. Maybe she'll be reluctant to comfort me in the future if I manage to drag this out into awkward land.

"It was okay," I lied. "She sent me a really nice Louis Vuitton purse."

Pari lifts her eyebrows. She takes her hands back and folds them in her lap. I'm sorry to break the spell. "That doesn't seem like your style."

"Oh, it's not. But I was able to sell it for, like, three grand. Covered a bunch of bills while I was still trying to find a job. Mom was pissed when she figured it out."

"It's not your fault she chose so poorly."

Though Pari's sniffing disdain is quieter than Nikki's tendency to drop f-bombs, they have similar opinions about my mom. "I'd offer you a trip to Alaska, but that would just be punishing you. And you've been nothing but nice to me. I don't know why some nice lesbian hasn't snapped you up already."

"I have a tendency to choose badly. I have before." She shakes her head, looking down at her hands. "I have every reason in the world to be nice to you."

It's like the world cants. It twists just a little off its axis. She didn't say anything creepy, she didn't leer at me. But I know. I absolutely know, like there's some sort of gravity between us, that she would . . . she would give anything. To me. If I wanted her to. I'm not even sure that would have been true a week ago, but now it is.

The insides of my elbows tingle. I don't know whether to giggle or melt into a puddle, which is the strangest thing in the world. I don't like women. I mean, I hardly like men even, for all the fuss it's worth, but I've never looked at a woman and thought, *I'd like to climb all over her.* I'm not there now, but I . . . I could get there.

So I push all this back to where it started. "You don't have to sweet-talk me. I'll be nearby when you're on Skype. Whenever you want."

She takes a deep breath, and it's like she sucks the hint of attraction back into herself. Her shoulders straighten, and she's a new person. "I believe I'll do it now. They're still up. The longer I think about this, the more I'll dread it."

"Do you have to tell them? I mean, they're a long, long way away."

Her laugh is short and bitter. She slides off the barstool, though she snatches the bowl of strawberries to take with her and also fishes a bottle of mineral water from the fridge. "Trust me. For my mother, the only thing worse than a gay daughter is a daughter who's hidden her marriage. I'm going to call. I'll let you know when I need you to come in."

"I'll keep an ear open."

I eat my lunch while I wait, first working through my toast. Five bites for each section gives me a sense of satisfaction. I eat one berry at a time, mindful of the way they burst between my teeth and their juices paint my mouth. Nourishment can be enjoyable, I tell myself.

I'm listening for Pari with every cell of my body. I want to be able to rush in there and rescue her, but I don't even know what I'm walking into. Will her parents be reluctant but generally accepting? Will they curse her? I don't like that idea.

Long, that's what it turns out to be. Pari is in her bedroom for more than three hours. Sometimes I hear her voice rise, and sometimes I think I hear her crying, but it's all in her language. She never asks me to come in, so I don't feel free to go. It's as if there's a spell on me.

I go to my room to wait, and theoretically I have my tablet to play games on, but I don't really see the colorful gems sliding around the screen.

I'm trying to imagine Pari's face. She's turning her whole life upside down, even at the same time that she's just trying to hold the pieces together. I think she's braver than I've ever been. The path of least resistance hasn't failed me yet. Well, it did for a little while, but then I pulled out of that.

When she finally asks for me, I jump fast enough that my feet get tangled in the throw blanket I've had over my lap. I mutter as I kick it away, trying not to curse even though I'm so anxious I've got a sledgehammer for a heart.

I pause at the threshold of Pari's bedroom, a little nervous. Okay, a hell of a lot of nervous. My hands shake when I push open the door.

Pari's folded in her office chair at the desk. She's arranged it up against a wall with a window. Though this side doesn't look out on the ocean, there are still a pretty blue sky and palm trees waving in a breeze. Pari's desk is sleek maple with cabinets on both ends. Her laptop has two faces pressed into the screen, as if they're trying to peer through the glass and see me before I even come into view.

Pari has a smile on her face, but she also has her knees tucked up under her chin and her arms wrapped around them. The fingers of one hand circle her other wrist, as if she's afraid of letting go even the littlest bit. "Hi, sweets. Come meet them."

*Sweets.* It sounds odd, but I roll with it. I grab the wing chair next to her bed and drag it over. I'm not going to buzz and bye, abandoning her when she looks so fragile. Her eyes are rimmed in red. I squeeze her foot briefly. "Hi. I'm Rachel Fizel."

The woman on the other end of the connection scowls. "She said your name. Can you remember ours?"

A test, already. Lovely. I move my mouth into a smile. "Sadashiv Jugnu and Niharika Sadashiv."

"Her pronunciation is terrible," Pari's father says directly to her. "She tried."

"I sent you that perfectly nice doctor's information, and you can't even try? For me?" That was from Pari's mother. Niharika is a beautiful woman, and it's easy to see where Pari gets her bold cheekbones and strong nose from. She has Pari's eyes as well, though they seem a little more gray than green. Perhaps that's from the Skype connection.

"I have tried, *Amma*. Many times." The skin around Pari's eyes is so dark that she seems bruised. Maybe that's on the inside. She rests a hand on my shoulder. "Rachel has a master's degree."

"But she works as a secretary!" Niharika screeches.

"At a film studio," I volunteer. Shit. Shit, shit, shit. I should have explained this earlier. Now I'm here living in this woman's house and I didn't give her all the information to tell her parents. "Technically my position is assistant producer."

"What?" chime all three voices at once. They pivot to look at me.

"You didn't say it was a studio," Pari says. Her gaze flicks to the screen and back again. "Just the name of the place. You said they're in entertainment."

"They are?" I volunteer hopefully. "Just . . . the movies kind of entertainment."

"You don't even properly know what she does for a living," Niharika says with disgust in her tone. Her nose wrinkles.

I don't like talking about this because I'm not where I wanted to be. Where I'd meant to be when I left school. "I got the job through one of my film professors. He knew a friend who was hiring. I'm an assistant producer, but all I *do* is secretary things. And the studio is work-for-hire. It's not considered a *real* studio. Not really. But there's . . ." I cough and heat attacks my cheeks. "There's room for upward mobility. In my field."

Pari's eyes don't narrow, but they . . . tighten? She's watching me, and I'll hear about this later, but for now she's letting it go rather than interrogate me in front of her parents.

"What good is improvement room if you're not even taking it?" Sadashiv leans in closer. "I worked from the time that I was ten to give my family a better life. To send Pari to America so she could have what she wants. And what she wants is a wisp of a blonde who has a job far below her studies? Why?"

Pari laces our hands together. It's only when she lifts them above the level of the camera, to display in the picture, that I realize it's just for show. I swallow. She brings our combined hands to her mouth and kisses my knuckles. The kiss is as light as fairy wings, and as reverent as taking mass. The way she looks up at me makes my stomach swoop. "She's the most positive person I've ever met, Papa." She looks back at the screen. "Not blindly positive though. She's hopeful even through the darkness she carries with her. You're going to admire her, *Amma*. Just give her a chance."

The darkness I carry? I don't like that part. Who would? I mean, she's probably right, but that doesn't matter as much as making those scowls on her parents' faces ease at least a little. Which they have.

"When will the wedding be?" Niharika crosses her arms over her chest and asks with an extra handful of displeasure sprinkled over the top.

Pari squeezes my hand, and I can feel my hope as if it were a radio wave between them. "We aren't going to make a big deal of it. We're meeting at the courthouse on Wednesday."

"No! Absolutely not." Niharika slashes a hand through the air so decisively that the camera wavers. "Already this will be . . ." She lets the sentence fade, and I breathe a sigh of relief for Pari's heart. There are only so many words that a daughter's feelings can ignore. "You will have a real marriage."

"A traditional wedding?" Pari seems doubtful. "I don't think that's wise."

"You would ignore even more of our traditions?"

"No, *Amma*—"

"We can have a big wedding. Well. Bigger than the courthouse, at least." The words fly out of my mouth before I think them through. But the moment Pari's mother gasps and claps her hands, I know I've made the right choice.

Pari turns to me with her eyes going huge. "You don't know what you're getting into," she whispers.

"It'll be fine." I bump my shoulder against hers. "I can have a white dress this way. I've never had a reason to wear a fancy dress."

"Not ever?"

"I skipped prom. I've worn nice dresses, but never a ball gown."

We're in our own little world again somehow. I know on one level that Pari's parents are avidly watching us, but I'm not paying attention to them. Pari's hand is hot in mine, and she's rubbing my knuckles with her thumb. I don't think she realizes, but I do. I realize with every inch of my hand. I'd pull away from the way it's making me feel, but Sadashiv and Niharika would wonder at our cracks.

That's what I tell myself, at least.

"You don't want a full Hindu wedding, Rachel. They're huge. All my family from all over will come. Multiday event."

"Even if you're marrying a woman?" I ask gently.

Her mouth opens, then shuts. She licks her lips, and I can see that she's breathing very deeply, just trying to hide it as best she can. "*Amma?*"

"They will come." Niharika is as self-assured as an empress. "If I tell them I approve, they will come. At the very least, to yell at us all for the disgrace of it."

"I don't want you to be disappointed in me," Pari says. The words are vulnerable, but she has that cool front on again.

"The wedding will help."

"You know your mother's intentions for you and your brothers," Sadashiv adds.

"We can do it," I say again.

"Less than one hundred guests," Pari says as crisply as if she's negotiating with a car salesman.

Niharika responds in exactly the same manner. "Anything less than three hundred and everyone will talk about how your father and I are trying to hide you."

"One fifty."

"Two."

I raise my hand. "Does that count my guests? Because I'll only have about twenty, at the outside."

"Only twenty family members?" Niharika looks at me with confusion knitting her brows.

I squirm a little. "Um. Twenty with family and friends."

"One seventy-five," Niharika says to Pari, and I feel like I've somehow given her bonus guest slots. Maybe she'll like me better for it?

Pari doesn't roll her eyes, but she squeezes my hand. "Deal. Six weeks from now?"

Niharika shakes her head. "You give me no time!"

Pari crosses her arms over her chest, which has the added effect of plumping her breasts up. I'm sure her parents don't notice, so I try not to as well. But she's endowed. There's no denying that. "Six weeks. I'm not giving on this."

Niharika's jaw sets, and it's apparent exactly where Pari got her determination. "I'll check the numbers and see if I can make it work."

"You *will* make it work. Less than seven weeks or I'll cancel it all."

"So willful," Niharika says. "I didn't raise you this way." But she doesn't seem unhappy either. It's like she's hiding a level of pleasure or pride. It's unfamiliar to me, so I have a hard time nailing it down.

Pari shrugs, but the tension in her shoulders eases a little. "Blame it on America if you want."

"I do." Niharika sighs, and Sadashiv hugs her shoulders with one arm. "I'll book my ticket and let you know when you, or she"—she adds, flicking a fast glance at me—"can pick me up from the airport."

"Okay, *Amma*."

"I'll be there in two weeks," she says with a sharp nod.

"*Amma*, what? No!" Pari lunges toward the screen, but it's too late. Her parents—or particularly Niharika—have already ended the call.

I stare at the computer. "Did she mean that? The two weeks?"

"Most assuredly." Pari hits the button, trying to call them back, but they aren't picking up. The digital ring goes on and on.

"So she's going to be in California for a month?"

"I knew she'd want to be very involved with the arrangements, but I didn't expect this."

I'm not doing so well at the breathing thing. "Will she . . . will she get a hotel room?"

Pari looks at me. Her eyes are filled with equal measures concern and panic. "I'm sorry, Rachel." She folds both my hands in hers.

"That's a no. Where will she stay?"

"Here. She'll stay here."

# chapter

Five

The next two weeks aren't exactly easy, but they go pretty quickly. My commute to the studio is faster from Pari's condo, not because it's any closer than my place on the other side of San Sebastian, but because I have easy freeway access. Pari works even longer hours than me, so she isn't always home when I come in, but things are slightly different in the way that's proof of another person living in the same sphere. The curtains left open instead of closed. The dishwasher having been run and magically full of clean dishes that I didn't have to hand wash. Groceries lined up neatly in the fridge.

Pari shops for us—or has a service do the shopping, I'm not quite sure—almost exclusively at Whole Foods and Trader Joe's. I absolutely adore the variety of food she keeps on hand. Every basic staple ingredient for the pantry, plus a wide range of perfectly ripe in-season fruit. It's like living in foodie heaven, except she isn't obnoxious about it.

My favorite Pari-sourced treats are dried mango slices. I nibble them slowly, the better to enjoy each bright bite. I'm curled up on the chaise-style end of the couch with the mangoes and a tumbler of ice water on the ottoman next to me while I watch TV.

"No! Annalise, you don't need another orphan!" I resist throwing a mango slice at the giant flat-screen. It'll probably stick, and then I'll feel all weird about cleaning the glass. What if I use the wrong product and ruin it forever? Better to wrinkle my nose and groan.

"What was that?" Pari calls from the kitchen.

"Nothing." I snuggle deeper into the couch as if it can hide how juvenile I am.

Pari appears in the archway. Energy burns off her. "You weren't talking to me?"

I hit Pause on the On Demand. "No, but would you like me to talk to you?"

"No. Yes. That is . . ."

"Is everything ready for your mom?" And no, I am very intentionally *not* thinking about the fact that we've hauled my dresser and a few other items into Pari's bedroom. The rest we figured we'd pawn off as being in the spare bedroom because we've called it my office. It isn't like six years of school and a year in a studio apartment have given me much chance to accumulate the detritus of life.

"Yes. I have fresh sheets to put on your bed in the morning. All the foods she likes. Her favorite chai."

"Are *you* ready?"

"Not in the least." The words explode from Pari like rockets at the Chinese New Year. "It was so hard to tell her I'm gay. To have *that* talk. I had a year before I saw her in person to let it sink in. I thought I would have the same about marrying a woman. One step at a time. Then you agreed to a wedding, which was frightening enough, but now I've only had two weeks to adjust to her knowing. Tomorrow I have to pick her up and look at her looking at me, knowing that her daughter is twisting her dreams."

Part of me wants to hold my arm out and have Pari come snuggle up beside me, but she doesn't really seem like the snuggling type. So I push my snack away and go to her instead. I hold her shoulders. It seems like she'll vibrate apart in moments, and she isn't quite looking at me.

I flex my knees so I can duck into her line of sight. "Hey. It's going to be fine."

"Sure. Yes. I'm certain."

I can tell it's only rote assurance. The kind of thing women are trained to say, the kind of thing I say all the time. "You know what this calls for?"

She doesn't actually answer, but she finally looks at me instead of somewhere over my left shoulder.

"It means we're going out for tequila and dancing."

I've worked a smile out of her. Her cheeks go round. "Make it gin, and you can count me in."

She's a woman of her word. Once we're at my favorite almost-local club, she strides right for the bar and waves down the bartender. I take my time working through the crowd. It's only a half-hour drive to get here, and it's a little bit of an adjustment from lying on the couch in my PJs. Pari has cleaned up seriously well. She's tossed on one of those dresses that shows off her amazing curves, and run some mascara through her already-sable lashes.

I don't feel like I've made the same evolution. I tug up the belt loop of my skinny jeans and tug down the hem of my halter top to try to get them to meet in the middle over the two inches of bare skin showing. I normally don't wear the combo together. I like this top because it makes me look like I have something like cleavage with its plunging neckline, but I don't want to be distracted by tummy pooch. At least I managed to find the time to do a French braid so the bend from the hair tie that held my ponytail all day isn't as obvious.

I catch up to Pari at the bar. The crowd means that I have to slide in right next to her. She is made of softness. Does she notice my pointy angularity? I try to hold my shoulders in tighter.

"Talk quick," she says. "The bartender is bringing my drink, but then he'll probably try to run away. He seems like a rabbit."

"He's busy." Even as we watch, a woman with a crisp undercut in her white-blonde hair tries to wave him down, pointing at the taps next to him.

"Such an optimist," Pari says, but she's smiling, so it feels fine.

When the bartender drops off her drinks—yes, plural, because he lines up two—I take the hint and order a vodka and Diet Coke.

"I'm glad we took an Uber," I sigh once I take the first sip. "That tastes way too good to stop at one."

"Do you drink much?"

It is so freaking weird that we're still at that stage of getting to know each other. Come to think of it, it's probably something we should have mentioned before diving in. But I shake my head. "Not usually."

"Me neither. I can't abide the lack of control."

"Me, it's kind of the opposite. I like it a little too much. I feel like I could drop off the earth."

"That seems extreme."

I laugh to make it a joke. "I'm an extreme person sometimes. At least in my head. If I start drinking, part of me is convinced that I would be on skid row in 2.4 hours, begging for change for another bottle of Hpnotiq."

"Well, don't worry." Pari nudges her shoulder into mine. We're both bare. Her skin is like silk, even softer than mine. I want to snuggle into her. "You're in my circle now. I'll take care of you."

"You won't let me hit skid row?"

"Nope. I'll even buy you all the peculiar blue liquor you want."

"I'm pretty sure that's enabling," I say between giggles.

"You're probably right. We should try to avoid that fate." She knocks back the bottom half of her first drink and picks up her second. "Let's try to find a table. I want one near the dance floor so I can watch for any baby dykes."

I follow her through the packed room. She doesn't push anyone out of her way, but she somehow gets a path opened for her. She's got presence. "Is that what you like?"

"What?" She looks back at me over her shoulder. Her hair is a dark frame for her questioning face.

I have to shout a little. "Baby dykes. Is that your type?"

She runs a fairly good chance of finding one here, though maybe just one. Killy's is a nightclub run by some athlete or another. The clientele is varied in that most excellent California way, with everyone who's anyone and who also has ten bucks to drop on a beer.

I don't like the strange little feeling that knots under my breastbone. My fingertips lift to rub there, but it doesn't help. I never drop my smile, but Pari looks at me as if she has some kind of inside track to what I'm thinking anyway.

"No," she finally replies. "They're fun to look at, but my life is a little too complicated to break in anyone new right now. They always come with drama when they're that young, even if they think of themselves as drama-free. I've been there already. Taneisha was enough."

Taneisha. Her ex-girlfriend has a name. And probably a face and a personality too. I don't know if I want to know more or not. Pari leads us closer to the music end of the huge setup. I'm not sure what kind of alchemy she uses, but three women leave a table as we approach, and they say we can have it. I drag my chair close to Pari's. This near to the dance floor, the thumping bass beat makes things difficult to hear, and I want to know more.

"Then what is your type? Now?"

I don't know why I'm insisting on the topic, until she slides a glance at me. "Beautiful women. Smart women. I do have a thing for blondes."

My heartbeat trips, and I know it's that right there. I needed a hit of appreciation. It's probably not fair of me. In a way it's using her, because I've pushed her into the corner of admitting that she finds me attractive, and I'm not going to give her anything in return, not really. Even though in this moment she's so beautiful that I can barely look straight at her. The flashing lights off the dance floor pick lines of color out in her dark hair. Her eyes seem to glow. Her dress has a neckline that doesn't plunge like mine, but it doesn't need to at all. Her breasts are so perfect that they only need the barest underscore for everyone to drool over her.

I admire her. I appreciate her body. That's not the same thing as actually wanting her.

So why am I not backing away?

It's Pari who backs off, who looks away with a miniscule shake of her head that I pretend not to see. It's easier. I usually do choose the easy way out, after all.

Until I have no easy way left.

I shift in my chair and also pretend that I'm not a thousand percent aware of the precise number of inches between her thigh and mine. I finish off my first drink. It hits me quickly.

Probably because I never got around to eating dinner. I had it planned down to the macronutrient, but I forgot to throw my salad together. I kept pushing it off and pushing it off and nibbling on a piece of mango. Instead we'd gone out.

All hail the Uber. I'd have made a shitty designated driver for the night, because I don't say a word about my lack of sustenance. I drink my vodka instead. Happily.

I suggested this night out for Pari's benefit, but it isn't as if I'm without nerves about her mother's arrival too. I need the time to unwind.

"Have you been here before?"

Pari shakes her head. "Nightclubs are so loud. They hurt my ears after a while."

"That's why I picked this place." I point up toward the balcony, which is walled off with plexiglass. The place is built in an old-fashioned dance hall, and the balcony rings the entire room. It's an entirely different vibe up there. The windows keep everything quiet, and it's all comfortable couches and dark corners between mazes of velvet curtains. "We can go up there if it gets too loud for us. Or we can dance until we drop. Your choice."

"My choice?"

"Sure." I shrug. "I figure you're the one who's melting down. You're the one who gets to choose our night."

"I am not melting down," she says with astonishment in her voice. It's kind of adorable.

"Okay."

"I was a little upset."

"Understandably so." I take a sip of my drink. My fingertips are chilled by the glass. "What should I expect? Will she be nice to me?"

"She'll be polite at the very least. It's her disappointment I'm scared of. How about you?" She's deflecting. Done with talking about herself, and that's fine. "How is your mother going to take the news that you're marrying a woman?"

"I already told her. The whole conversation took about five minutes."

"Wait, what?" Pari's eyes are wide and catch the flicker of a strobe light. She swirls the ice in her glass. "Even if she's progay, how is that even possible? Five minutes?"

I shrug. Three feet in front of us is a hetero couple who are dancing like it's prom and the chaperones turned their back. Her arms are wrapped around his shoulders, and his hands are shoved in the ass pockets of her tiny shorts. I don't understand how people dance like that. I've done it, because dates have dragged me, and it obviously made them happy. But it's never made me hot and bothered the way the two in front of us seem to be.

"It was easy. I said I'd met someone, that you were nice, and we were getting married. Told her an invitation would be in the mail. Six weeks is tight notice for her though."

"She doesn't have any questions about me?"

"Your name and what you do."

I think Pari makes a little noise, because her mouth shapes into a circle, but I have no chance of hearing it. Not with the blazing cavalcade of noise that is the sound system. Maybe she feels bad for me. I kinda want her to. I like sympathy. Doesn't everyone? But this night isn't for me. I wave my hand. "It's no big deal. She's just always been like that. She's got a really hands-off parenting style."

"There's hands-off, and then there's neglect."

I like the way she's full of cold anger on my behalf, but it makes me squirmy at the same time. I've probably gone too far, told too much truth. She doesn't need my mess on top of her own. "It's not like that. She's just always let me live my own life. It's made me independent. And besides, you should be grateful. If I had parents breathing down my neck, I might not have agreed to this scheme."

"Fair point." She raises her glass in a small salute, then finishes it off. "Can we get me another one of these?"

I wave down a waitress, and this time I just ask for a diet soda because I can barely feel my cheeks now. I'll have another drink in a minute. Pari's gin and tonic comes quickly.

I cast around for conversation. "Do you like hedgehogs?"

Pari laughs at me, but it's entirely good-natured. "What? Where in the world did that come from?"

"I follow this stupid cute hedgehog with vampire teeth on Instagram." Heat attacks my cheeks and the back of my neck. I tug my shirt down. "Fine. I'll stop trying to act like the social hostess for the night. You pick the conversation."

"What were you watching earlier? At the house. On TV."

"You haven't seen it before?" Oh, she's going to regret asking. The floodgates open, and I start gushing about how smart the show is.

That gets her started on a web series that she's watched and that she'd initially loved until it went downhill. Before we know it, we're three drinks in and I've accidentally ordered two more vodkas.

I feel good when she stands up and drags me onto the dance floor. We dance independently but like we're tied in tandem. I shake my ass to the beat, and I know Pari is watching. I feel like I'm being naughty, trying to get her attention, but it's only fair, because she has mine.

She has my focus in a way no one has before. Or maybe I'm exaggerating, but at the very least it's been so long I can hardly remember the feeling. It's not that I'm asexual, but I'm not exactly comfortable with the whole package either. The rush starts in my stomach with a flip and spreads outward from there.

Maybe it's just being the center of attention. I know I have a problem with that. I like Pari's eyes on me. I like knowing she's looking.

I let her catch my hand. The music strokes through me, and I think it's increasing the feeling that's making my stomach all wiggly. It's thumping tripwires in my brain. I like it. I like her hand wrapped in mine. She laces our fingers together. It's just dancing. There's nothing wrong with this.

We spin together, then apart. She lets me have space. Room to breathe. I feel like a diamond on a chain that she's showing off.

I'm laughing when we tumble off the dance floor. "Want to go upstairs?"

We find a small cushioned bench behind a curtained nook. Dirty, naughty, wrong things have happened here. I know it as I lean against the satin cushions. My toes tingle. I sit and tuck my feet up under my butt, knees pointing to one side. Pari sits at the other end of the couch, but she doesn't settle in. She waves down a new waitress and orders us another round of drinks plus a basket of french fries.

My mouth waters. God, I have such problems. I decide I'll have ten fries. That's a reasonable amount without denying myself. At least I'm not having daiquiris, even though I miss them desperately.

When the fries show up, they're in a tiny shopping cart sized just right for a Barbie. I laugh as I take one. "This is ridiculous!"

Pari puts two fingers on the miniature red bar and pushes it across the plate between the dishes of ketchup and mustard. "Just a few potatoes to pick up."

"Okay, *you're* ridiculous."

"It's got wheels! It's meant to be pushed." We're both dying of laughter.

We melt into each other, shoulder against shoulder. I like contact. I like contact with her.

I think I'm drunk.

She kisses me.

At first I almost don't know what's going on. Her mouth feels so much different than a man's. It's a softer approach, one that's barely a breath across my lips, and then she's drinking my laughter.

I jolt. Low-down deep in my body. A hard clench that shoves my lungs and squeezes my pussy. It's not a feeling I've had before, and if this is what everyone else gets all the time, I can see why they turn their lives upside down for certain people.

But it's so much. My head is spinning. I lift my hands, but it's not as if I'm going to touch her. If only having her lips on mine does this to me, tripping over my mouth like a butterfly dances over flowers, I can't imagine touching her face like I want to. She tastes like salt and the juniper bitters of gin. Is this what it's supposed to be like?

She pulls away first. Of course she does. I want to chase her lips with mine. I don't. I'd chase her to Mars for only scraps of attention. I fold my hands in my lap and try to focus on the space beyond our cloth cubbyhole.

"I'm sorry," she says.

"I know." I cover my face with the hands I almost used to grab her. "I mean it's fine. Really."

"It's not. I shouldn't have done that."

"We'll pretend it never happened."

*I* wake up way too early the next morning. The sunlight hurts my eyes, but that's probably more to do with all the vodka I drank last night. There had been another round after the kiss, as if Pari and I were both pretending that it was all fine and nothing strange had happened.

It's all I can do to keep my head on straight. I draw my knees up and sit cross-legged as I try to balance my throbbing temples between my fingertips.

I have to come out of the room eventually.

I take my time.

Pari is in the kitchen, standing in front of that beautiful center island. She's wearing a silk blouse and a pencil skirt as if she's going into work. I have a moment of panic punch me in the stomach, and it isn't as if my tummy was feeling that great to begin with.

"Are you going somewhere?" Fear makes me flighty, until I realize what I'm doing. I can't throw a fit over feeling abandoned when I'm the one who wants to back off.

It can be mutual backing off. That would be okay. I'm pretty sure.

She gives a little shake of her head. She's chopping herbs with fast, efficient motions and a knife that looks entirely too big for the task. "Not until it's time to get my mother."

"Oh," I say lamely. "I didn't think you'd get dressed until later." Because that's what I'd do. But she's not me. *Duh.*

"Would you like breakfast?"

I put a hand over my stomach, like that's going to keep my insides where they belong. "I don't know if I can handle it."

Her knife stills. Pari tongues her bottom lip, then looks up at me. "Trust me?"

"Sure." I'm surprised by how quickly I answer. I don't trust myself, much less anyone else. But I want to trust her. Surely that should count, right?

"Sit, sit." She waves at the barstool and bustles around getting ingredients out.

She pulls a blender from a hideaway cabinet and throws ice and bananas and a couple other things in. The result is thick and white and frothy. She pours it into a tall, skinny glass and nudges it toward me.

"Um."

Her smile is gentle. "You said you trust me."

I have no way to take back my words, and I don't think I want to. Probably. "Can I have a straw?"

"A straw?"

"Long? Skinny? Tubular?"

"I think I may . . ." She digs in a drawer next to the sink before triumphantly waving a half-empty pack of neon straws. "From when Heidi brought her boy over."

She holds them out to me, and I pick a bright-blue one. It goes well with the pale yellow of my drink. "Who's Heidi?"

"We work together. Her son is four. He likes *My Little Pony* and *Star Wars*."

"Smart kid."

I drink. The banana is smooth and sweet. Frothiness keeps it light. There's a bite of ginger that settles my stomach. The sugar hits me quickly. I manage to suck it all down in short order.

I don't realize my hands are shaking until I tuck my fingertips between my thighs. My lounge pants are thin cotton, and dampness from the glass's condensation sinks through immediately.

"What is it?" I don't know what Pari sees in my expression to make her ask.

"I took food from someone else without knowing the calorie count." I take a deep breath. "And it doesn't feel all freaky. Not too freaky, at least."

"I'm glad."

I like her smile. It makes me feel clean. "I'm going to have to tell my therapist about this."

"She'll be proud of you. I am."

I blush and look down at my hands against my striped PJ pants. *Christ.* "It's silly."

"It's not." She reaches across the island and takes my hand from my lap. Compared to my fingers, hers are scalding hot. "If it's a new step for you, then it's really important. I bet your therapist wouldn't want you belittling your progress."

"She wouldn't."

I don't know why Pari needs me. I don't know what I'm doing here. She's too fucking nice. "Has your mom met any of your girlfriends before? Taneisha?" I make myself say the name with a straight face, not giving in to the temptation to sneer.

"She did when Taneisha and I were friends. When she was . . . with her husband still." She shrugs eloquently. "It was all very complicated. I assisted her through a rough patch in her life. *Amma* met her. Then we dated. Then we didn't."

"What did your mom think of her?"

"That I shouldn't mess around with straight girls." She makes a face. "Though she didn't use those words."

I nibble on the inside of my lip. More proof that last night's kiss shouldn't have happened. "How can I help today?"

"If you could go over your room and make sure it doesn't look . . . personal? Move around whatever you'd like in my room, as if you really were moved in."

"Are you sure this is going to work?"

"No idea." Her accent seems to be getting thicker as she gets tenser. "But I have to try or this all may fall apart."

I go to the airport with her. I'm not entirely sure how it happens. One minute I'm helping get the rooms straightened out, and the next I'm saying, "Sure, I'll go. Why not?" and getting in Pari's little Audi so we can zip off to LAX. If by "zip off" I mean "sit at the exit, trying to get off the freeway for close to an hour."

California has its occasional downsides.

LAX is currently under construction too, which means navigating our way to the international arrivals involves sliding past plastic sheeting and precarious-looking drywall. I worry the side of my thumb between my teeth. "Is it really self-centered of me to say I hope she doesn't hate me?"

"A little bit. This is kind of my entire familial relationship structure about to be tested," Pari replies dryly.

"Thought so." Except we grin at each other. Maybe it's not going to be so bad.

A crowd spills through the gates, and a lot of them are middle-aged Indian women, but only one is Niharika Sadashiv. I know her the minute I see her, mostly because she looks like a more mature version of the woman next to me. And not-that-mature as it is.

Her hair is down around her shoulders in a style similar to Pari's, though her mother's is even darker. Closer to true black. Her long, pink tunic looks like it would have been incredibly comfortable for her flight, especially with the wide-legged pants she has on beneath it. I don't know what the style is called, something that's unmistakably Indian and yet has a modern flare. It probably helps that Niharika is slim and elegant.

I hope I look half as good when I'm in my fifties.

Pari waves, her hope living in her every cell. It radiates out of her like heat from a star that could explode any moment. I hope this works for her. All the rest of it aside, she's taking such a huge risk by bucking her family's marriage expectations. My heart bursts with pride and admiration.

Niharika hugs her daughter close. They're the same height. Pari buries her face in her mother's shoulder, and that's when the tears start. Pari's shoulders hitch once, then twice, then in a steady shaking stream.

I jump, reach over, and pet her back in slow strokes. I avoid Niharika's hands at Pari's shoulders. I don't know this woman enough to touch her, enough to interrupt her connection with her daughter. I can't *not* help Pari though.

I do my best to block them from the rest of the oncoming crowd, but people are mostly giving them space anyway. We're an island of female emotion in an intersection between worlds. The scents of cardamom and masala wrap around us. I think they might be coming from Niharika. I'm not sure.

I wish I had someone, anyone, who held me like that. Who didn't start nudging me away after it had been too long. Who I didn't start pulling away from because maybe they'd get tired of me.

It's more than fifteen minutes before Pari finally lifts her head. I look away while she wipes her eyes and then her nose on a tissue Niharika hands her.

"My poor *magal.*" Niharika strokes Pari's hair away from her sticky cheeks. The next words are in Tamil that I have no hope of following, though I do catch the word *appa.*

Whatever it is, it's enough to make Pari smile. It's not a huge smile, just the tiniest curl of her lips, but God, it's enough. I can breathe again.

I step back, making sure I have one hand on the handle of Niharika's carry-on so it doesn't disappear with a stranger. I try not to be intrusive while they talk. Mostly that means not staring at them too hard. I use the time to figure out which baggage carousel we need to find, but that takes all of thirty seconds reading an electronic board.

"*Amma,* this is Rachel." Pari catches my hand and pulls me near.

I can't even imagine how nerve-racking this would be if Pari and I were actually in love. As it is, I think I probably crave Niharika's approval entirely too much. She looks me up and down slowly, and I'm perfectly aware that I'm medically still too skinny at the same time that I feel fat as a cow. It's a hideous combination. Seeing the silk tunic Niharika effortlessly wears makes me wish I'd worn something nicer than jeans rolled to my calves and an Old Navy blouse, even if I like the tiny pattern of anchors. I feel like a wrinkled mess, and I only had an hour-and-a-half drive. I have no idea how she looks so good after an incredibly long flight.

I put a hand out. "It's nice to meet you, Mrs. Sadashiv."

"Call me Niharika." Her voice is lower than Pari's and sweetly rounded. She has less of a British crispness to her words.

"Niharika," I echo.

"No, Niharika."

I repeat it, and this time I must have gotten it close enough to right, because she nods. I feel like I've hurdled a high jump.

"Let's go get your bags, *Amma*," Pari says, and they go.

They walk arm in arm, heads leaning together. I follow them with the rolling suitcase, half laughing at myself and half envying their connection.

Life is so freaking strange sometimes.

We're waiting at the baggage claim, listening to the creaking clack of the belt, when Niharika abruptly grabs my left hand and holds it up.

"No ring," she says in full-on accusatory tones.

We're busted. So freaking busted. My eyes go wide. My stomach drops to my flip-flops. I trade a glance with Pari, who looks just as messed up as I feel.

She can only make an inarticulate noise, and I think I'm making something pretty similar. It's hard to tell with the way my ears ring.

Niharika drops my hand and then holds up her daughter's in the same way. "No ring on you either. Why don't either of you have engagement rings?"

"*Amma*, engagement rings are Western," Pari manages to choke out. I'm so relieved that she does, because I have no idea what I could have said. I'm still stuck in "high-pitched whine" mode.

"As if marrying a woman is not Western?" Her chin lifts. Her eyebrows are graceful arches that frame her brown eyes. "Which of you is to be the man?"

Pari sputters. Her cheeks turn bright red beneath her brown color. "*Amma*! You can't ask that!"

"I am not asking how you—" Niharika flaps a hand. "Do the things. I have arrangements to make. These are important details."

Pari covers her face with her hands. "I'm going to die. I'm going to fall into the floor and be gone forever."

"Take me with you," I deadpan.

"Neither have rings. It makes me think both of you wish to be the man."

I raise my hand. "I'll take a ring. I like rings. Rings are pretty."

Oh God. What in the world have I gotten myself into?

"Good," Niharika says with another one of those nods that I'm starting to think are her trademark. "Tomorrow we go get you a ring."

Pari raises her hand too. "What if I say I want a ring too? What then?"

"Pfft. I raised you to be my daughter. Certainly you get a ring. We have two brides. Two rings. Lovely, pretty things, so everyone knows that my daughter is to be married now."

And there, right there . . . the laughter drops out of me. I wonder if maybe this is all a horrible, terrible idea. I have this feeling that I could maybe like Niharika. It doesn't feel right to be lying to her. I catch Pari's gaze, which is dark and troubled like maybe she's having similar thoughts.

But there's no backing out now. Not if Pari is going to stay in the US.

Two brides it is.

chapter

$\mathcal{S}$even

*I* am in over my head. I spend six hours sitting on the couch listening to Pari and her mother talk about every person in the world, and they're related to them all. When Niharika turns a smile on me and asks about my family, I panic. I'm half tempted to squeeze closer to Pari on the couch, but I don't know if that would be okay. Either to Pari or to Niharika. I fold my arms around my stomach instead.

"I have a really small family."

"How many siblings do you have?"

I glance at Pari. "None."

Maybe we should have gone over this earlier. I should have been briefed on the probable interrogation that was coming my way. Because no matter what kind expression Niharika has arranged her smile into, I know what this really is.

"How surprising," she says before sipping her chai. "And your mother? How many siblings does she have?"

"None. My dad had a brother." I lean toward Pari because at least I know her. She holds straight and steady, my rock. She pats my knee. "Their families took part in the post–World War II WASP diaspora. We're not very connected to our other family."

"The wasp diaspora?" Niharika's brows knit together. "I'm sorry, I do not know this event."

My first impulse is to scrunch smaller into the back of the couch. I pick up a red accent pillow and hold it in my lap instead. "Stupid joke. Sorry. My grandparents moved out to California in the fifties, after World War II. They settled in Pasadena and Wilshire. That's all I meant."

"And do they still live there?" Niharika is calculating. Upping my percentage of the guest count, I guess.

I shake my head. "No. They're gone now. It's just me and my mom and my uncle."

"And your uncle's family?" she prompts.

Except I have nothing to give her there either. Terry is as gay as can be and moved to San Francisco about thirty years ago. I love staying in his Castro District Victorian when I visit. "He's single."

"I see."

There goes my percentage of the invitations, crashing again. I almost feel like I should go find her a notebook and a set of colored pens so that she can make detailed notes. Maybe she needs one of those big flat maps that generals use to move mechanized units around on. We could set it up in the dining room. Instead of miniature tanks, we'd get her banquet tables and floral displays.

That isn't such a bad idea. I bet my buddy Tom could make it. He does a lot of stuff with his hands, including shaping surfboards. He might think it's funny.

"I have a lot of friends," I offer, feeling a little bit like that girl who doesn't have a date to homecoming and has to go with five girlfriends. Even if we're going to have fun, we all know it's not the same.

"Will your mother come to dinner soon?"

I look at Pari, who just shrugs. "There's a lot of ceremony that involves both sides of the families in a Tamil wedding. It might be a good idea to decide which parts we want to do."

I am such a fucking idiot. Why did I get any kind of excited over the idea? I know Mom won't show. She'll be busy. Plans that can't be broken. And then I'll get disappointed over her failure to show up for arrangements for a wedding that's *fake*, for Christ's sake. I wish Pari hadn't thrown this at me in front of her mother. "Can we talk about this later?"

Pari immediately nods. Her hand finds mine. Her bones are delicate across my knuckles. "Sure, no problem."

I smile at her. I flip my hand over so we're palm to palm. I want her to feel my relief, my appreciation. I can't seem to say anything, but that's fine. She knows. It's there in the way she's looking at me.

"I would like In-N-Out," Niharika announces. She stands and puts her teacup on a side table before brushing imaginary bits of nothing off the pink silk of her tunic.

"No, *Amma*. What?" Pari's completely taken aback and laughing at the same time.

Niharika lifts both hands. "Not for a burger. I want french fries and I want them 'animal style.'"

"How do you even know about that?" Pari is laughing, but she's also getting up and doing exactly what her mom wants. She's effortlessly put together as soon as she slips on Ferragamo flats with a grosgrain ribbon bow across the toes.

"The internet exists in India, young lady. We're not savages."

"I didn't mean that." She scoops up her purse and drags her thick hair back into a ponytail that lies down between her shoulder blades. "I meant what are you doing spending your time looking up fast food on the internet?"

"I can use my time however I like." Niharika looks at me, and I can't read her expression. It's pleasant. She's smiling, and her eyes aren't pinched. But there are depths in her eyes that I don't understand the same way that I feel like I understand Pari's. "Would you like to come with us?"

Can I say no? I can't tell. I look at Pari, but she mostly looks happy. I feel just the tiniest bit tossed to the wolves. I don't know how to interpret happy when it comes to what I should do. "No, thanks?"

Neither Niharika nor Pari look surprised or hurt or wounded by me declining, so my shoulders untighten a fraction.

"We'll be home in a little bit." Pari gives me a kiss on the cheek, and I don't flinch. "I may take her down to see the ocean."

"I don't know why," Niharika replies as she rolls her eyes. "She drags me there every time I visit. It's only water and sand that gets stuck beneath my clothes. I can see the ocean through the windows when I like!"

"It's a law. If you visit San Sebastian, you have to touch sand, or you're not allowed to come back next time," I say, and then I wish I could cram a fist in my jaw. Because seriously?

Except, thank God, Niharika laughs. "Maybe this explains it."

They leave in another bustle of rapid activity. The door shuts behind them. I stand in the foyer, breathing. Just breathing deep. My ears feel peeled from my skull, and I appreciate the sudden quiet.

Until the door pops open again. It's just Pari this time. She whirls in on a cloud of expensive perfume and envelops me in a tight hug.

"Thank you," she whispers against my ear. "You're being fantastic about this all."

I can't hold back the shiver. "You're welcome."

And then she's gone again, except I feel . . . warm all over. A smile curls around my mouth. I put the thumbs of loosely curled fists against my bottom lip.

Maybe . . . maybe this isn't going to be so bad.

chapter

Eight

Bedtime comes sooner than I expect. Niharika is tired when she gets back from In-N-Out and says good-bye for the night. It's early, but she's still on India time. I wonder when she's going to wake up. Probably before dawn. I hope she has a plan to deal with that.

Except *duh*, she probably does. She's been back and forth between here and her home more than once.

I spend the evening messing around on my laptop. I waste a lot of time on Tumblr and a little time on Facebook, and in the background I always have open a certain document. One I don't like to think about too much. It's Richard's, after all, not mine. He's a pretty decent guy considering most of the dude bros I meet in Hollywood, but he's just this close to self-imploding at any moment. Maybe every moment. Twenty years ago, he was a god of the movies. I even remember Courtney, the nanny who lived in our mother-in-law suite for my kindergarten year, having a massive, obsessive crush on him. That was when Richard was the kind of fresh-faced star who unironically graced wall-sized posters. Now he's a silver fox with substance abuse problems and a script that needs a whole metric fuck-ton of work before it's enough of a vehicle to drag him back from obscurity.

I only add a couple words to it at a time, because if I do it that way, I'm not actually working. It doesn't mean anything real.

Pari curls up on the other couch with her laptop. I don't ask, but I'm pretty sure she's working, trying to shove in what she can. Whatever the topic is, she's completely absorbed in it. She's changed into linen pajamas. The pants are loose, and the top is a button-down. She's left the top buttons undone, and I try not to watch the arch of her neck. Her brown skin looks especially warm and touchable against the pale-yellow pajamas.

I look at my keyboard and try to keep my gaze stuck there. Mostly, I succeed. It's awkward when I start getting tired. I flick over my touch screen slowly, as if each new image needs a half hour of inspection. I'm like a toddler who doesn't want to go to bed. At least I never rub my eyes with my fists.

I just stare at my screen until Pari claps her computer shut. I jump, but only on the inside. Outside, I think I keep cool.

"I need to go to sleep," she says. "*Amma* will be up early."

I nod. I keep nodding. I'm a stupid bobblehead doll, complete with big head and too small a body. "Sure. Sure."

"Will you . . . Are you coming later?"

"I don't plan to." I clap my hand over my mouth. It doesn't help. I squeak with laughter anyway. "Sorry. Probably bad timing."

Pari wrinkles her nose and sticks her tongue out at me.

"Is that an offer?" I tease, because apparently I like compounding bad taste with more bad taste.

That's enough to make her laugh though. I like the way it loosens her up. "If I'm ever offering to lick your pussy, trust me, you'll know. You'll know when I'm done too, when you've come so many times that your legs won't hold you up."

Not funny anymore. My head spins. I've never been talked to like that. I had a boyfriend when I was still in full-blown anorexia status who'd thought he was a dirty talker. Mostly that meant he liked to call me a slut. I'd let him because it made him happy and because I didn't really care. There was nothing he could say to me that was worse than what I already said to myself.

It hadn't been like this. I want to tell Pari to stop because I can't handle it, and I want to tell her to go on too. What else would she do to me? Is it actually about me, or is this something she'd say to any woman she flirts with?

I'm dying of excitement and embarrassment at the same time. Laughing it off is my only option. "So many promises over the years." I shake my head with mock sorrow as I get up. "So sad that no one ever manages to back up bragging like that."

"Never?" She tips her head to the side. Her feet are on the couch, and I'm standing above her, looking down. I can see a shadowy hint of cleavage beneath her pajama top, but that's it. She's still one of the most sensual people I've ever met. It breathes out of her. "You poor, neglected thing."

"I'm not neglected. I've gotten around." Maybe I'm warning her? *I'm a more terrible person than you think. Beware of me.*

"You could sleep with a hundred people, and it's not the same thing as sleeping with one who'll really spend the time messing you up." She stands, stretching her arms over her head, and I can't understand how these groundbreaking words are coming out of her mouth while she's just acting like it's no big deal at all.

I give the "heh" of a cranky retiree who wants to pretend they're still hip. I act as if it takes concentration to fold the lap blanket I've been using, and stack my phone on my laptop. I even wrap my power cord up. Because I'm obviously an idiot.

I follow Pari to the bedroom silently. If we were really a couple, this would be a thing we did all the time. A thing we'd do with laughter or kisses or with our fingers intertwined.

Have I slept with too many men? Was there really such a thing as too many? I wouldn't want to tell my number to anyone, so that was probably a bad sign to most people. I'd need a pen and paper to make sure I got them all. That was a bad sign even to me.

Most of them were in the great gray before. When I was a mess. When I wasn't healthy. Men liked my too-skinny body a lot. They liked the way my makeup was flawless every day then, and they didn't question whether I was okay when I felt compelled to get up from bed after sex to reline my lipstick. Or they liked it for a while, and then they didn't and were done with me. Or they didn't like it, and they said something, and then I was done with them. Because I needed to be flawless. I craved being flawless.

I've given up on perfection. I don't quite believe that no one could have it, because there are certain people . . . Ones I tried not to look at too closely. I didn't know what color of crazy the inside of their world is painted with. Sometimes I'm almost relieved when Pari is cool, when she makes those slightly cutting comments. At least I know what's up with her.

But I still took those cocks. I held them and let them in and fucked them.

None of them had made me really give a shit. No one had made me come except when my own fingers were on my clit. I figured it was just the way I was built. Anorexia nervosa and anxiety and a low-grade case of the frigids.

No big deal.

When Pari closes the door to her room behind us, it feels like a very big deal. I want to know what she'd do with her mouth.

This is so unfair of me. Pari isn't a step in my therapy. She's a human being who has a problem, and we're trying to solve our problems together. She's being incredibly generous as it is, lightening the burden of my student loans.

But thoughts are swirling in my head. Maybe it's time to step outside of my comfortable, safe space. Maybe I need to start knowing what really makes me tick. What turns me on.

Obviously, we can put dirty talk pretty high up on that list.

"Do you sleep on the left side or the right?" Pari's standing at the end of the bed, busying her hands with folding a shirt she left tossed over the end.

I shrug, but she's not looking at me. "Honestly? I'm kind of a sprawler. I'll try to contain myself, but I don't care which side."

The bed's a king, so I hadn't thought this would be so difficult. But it's not the same thing, standing in a room where it's the main feature, knowing you'll lie down on that mattress in moments with another person in arm's reach.

"Then I'd like to be on the right, because that's where I have my phone plugged in."

"Works for me."

I grab a pair of pajama shorts from my top drawer and go into the attached bathroom to change. I hate the way pants get wrapped around my legs and the sheets while I sleep. But even while I'm switching out my lounge pants for the shorts, I wonder if that's necessary. It's not like I'm panty-free, and it's not like Pari hasn't seen half-dressed women before. We're teasing like friends, but last night's kiss isn't any reason to be wired up or nervous around her.

I paw through my thoughts and feelings, trying to figure out why I'd hopped in here to change. I cringe when I finally find the reason: it's more about me than her. I'm still not comfortable being undressed around anyone.

Hi, my name is Rachel, and I'm one hundred percent messed up in the head.

Pari is in bed by the time I come out. She's turned off the overheads, and the nightstand lamps give the room a soft trickle of light. I hustle to the bed and slide in. The sheets are cool and smooth against my bare legs. I wiggle until I have the blanket tucked up over my shoulders. It's lightweight and the perfect counter to the slight chill of the air conditioning.

"So. Good night, I guess." I look up at the ceiling because I know without trying that rolling to my side and seeing Pari that close will be too much to handle.

"Thanks for doing this, Rachel."

I have to look, because I want to see the warmth that I hear in her voice. She's lying on her side, knees slightly tucked up. She makes a rounded mound under the blankets and sheets. Her hair is in a braid that curves over her throat.

I almost say, *It's nothing*, but that's an old habit trying to rear its head. "You're welcome."

"I'll make it up to you. I'll be the best wife you never meant to have." She grins. "Without all the emotional hard stuff."

She has no idea how much hard emotional stuff I wade through on a daily basis, but that's fine. "You already are."

We click off the lights. Silver moonlight spills in from the window near the study area, but it doesn't reach as far as the bed. We're swathed in darkness. I'm trapped between nervous giggles and the tense feeling of not wanting to move because it would shake the bed.

"Is this the part where we tell ghost stories?" Pari asks.

"What?" I have no idea what she's talking about.

"American sleepovers. When girls have them in movies, there are usually ghost stories."

I laugh, and it's definitely in the nervous-giggles category. I roll onto my side to face Pari and fold one hand under my pillow. "There're only ghost stories if some guy is standing outside with a knife."

"We're too many floors up. If anyone's outside the window with a knife, it's Spider-Man."

"I've always suspected Peter Parker was a creeper. I never understood that whole Mary Jane/Gwen Stacy thing."

"Don't forget Betty Brant too."

"Who?" I push up on an elbow. I think my eyes are adjusting, because I can at least see the outline of Pari's jaw and shoulder.

"Betty Brant. She worked at the *Daily Bugle*."

"And behold, a nerd appears."

"A nerd was always here. You just weren't looking."

The air between us thickens and catches in my throat. I hear something different in what could have been a joke. I'm not sure if she meant for it to be there. My response slips out before I have the chance to think twice about it.

"I'm looking now."

*Nine*

*I* wake up warm and cozy. The blankets are wrapped around me. I'm lying on my side, one hand curled under my pillow and the other on a curve that's soft and firm at the same time. I keep my eyes closed and nestle closer into the niceness. I smell coconut. Somewhere far away, I hear the distant thump of a helicopter's blades, but it's nothing to be worried about. A news copter or something.

Except, shit, it's not. It's knocking at the door.

Gasping, I sit straight up. Should I answer? It's Pari I've been nestled up against. We've both made our way toward the center of the bed—miles from the edge I started the night out clinging to.

I wiggle back to my side. The knocking comes again, but Pari doesn't hear it—or doesn't want to. She makes a grumpy noise and pulls the pillow over her head.

I poke her. "Hey. That's your mom."

"Nuh-uh."

"Yeah-huh." I shake her shoulder. She's glowing with the warmth of sleep. Part of me is tempted to pretend I don't hear anything and snuggle back under the blanket to join her.

The rest of me thinks that's absolutely batshit crazy.

I rake my hair back with my fingers, trying to get it to straighten into some sort of normalcy. It's not likely. I usually look similar to a scarecrow when I get up. The duck fluff that pretends to be my hair gets up to funny business while I sleep.

"Um. Hi," I say once I've cracked the door open.

Niharika has the hall light on. I squint. She's already dressed and completely put together, all the way down to a gold necklace and dangling earrings. "I've made breakfast. Come."

I don't know what it is about this woman, but I start to blindly obey her and follow her four steps down the hall before I realize. "Oh. I should probably wake up Pari." And go to the bathroom too, but there's no reason for me to say that part.

"Certainly. Come quickly though, dosas are best when they're fresh."

Dosas. Oh man. My mouth waters. I hustle back into the bedroom and, without thinking, I launch toward the bed, landing on my knees. "Pari! Pari, wake up, your mom cooked."

She grumbles and wiggles as if she's trying to get deeper under that pillow. I yank it away.

"What the hell?" she grouses.

"Dosas! She made dosas."

"So? I set the batter up for her last night."

Okay, so fine. This is not a big deal to her. I guess it's something like if an overly excited infant jumped on my bed and started squeeing at me about someone making pancakes. Pleasant, but not exactly worth making an idiot of myself over. "I happen to enjoy dosas."

She lifts a single, graceful eyebrow. "I'm beginning to see that. I'll make you dosas for Christmas, since they're all you think about."

I tickle her in retaliation. My fingers find the soft undersides of her armpits. She squeals, completely taken by surprise. "You brat!" she howls.

I have no mercy. She's writhing under me, and her hips jump as if she's trying to buck me off. But she's also laughing like mad, which makes it completely worth it. She tries to bat me away. I only tickle her harder, until she cries mercy.

"I need to pee," she says between peals of giggles.

"Promise you'll never make fun of me again."

"Never?" she asks, drawing the word into long syllables of doubt.

"Not ever." I put my serious face on again. "Especially not about food."

She somehow sees through me. "Oh. *Oh*. I said something really bad, didn't I?"

She pushes up to a sitting position, which makes me realize that I'm straddling her thighs. I scramble off her. I'm shaking my head even though it's not the first thing she's said to me about food. She's only human. No one can be perfect. I shouldn't expect so much. "No, not really. You didn't say anything."

She holds my shoulder. Her hand is hot, her fingers like individual brands. Maybe I'm allergic to her. "I won't tease about food again. I'm sorry."

"It's not a big deal." By which I mean I don't *want* it to be a big deal. Isn't that the same thing, more or less?

"I'm still sorry. It was insensitive."

"It really wasn't." I feel pinned by her kindness. It makes me squirm inside, so my next words explode like a gush from a broken faucet. "It's not even the food. I just don't like the idea that there's maybe something that you don't think I can control myself around. It just doesn't help that it's food."

She doesn't let go of me. It's only then that I realize I had *expected* her to let go. My life is ruled by a thousand and one expectations, and none of them ever turn out like I think they will. Instead she holds my other shoulder too. Her bright-green eyes bore into mine. I swallow and realize the back of my throat is stinging.

"I will never tease you about food or a lack of control again."

She means it. I can feel conviction pouring out of her and wrapping around me. I want to twist it up and tie it around my shoulders like kids do to make blankets into superhero capes. I would carry Pari's conviction with me forever if I could. This morning will have to be enough. I smile because it's all I can manage without bursting into sniveling tears.

"Time to go eat?" I ask, because that's easier than the tangle inside me.

"Yes. We better hurry up. *Amma* will be annoyed if they go soggy because we're being slow."

"You use this bathroom, then. I'll stop at the one in the hall."

"Deal."

We reconvene in the kitchen at almost the same moment. Niharika sits beneath the window, both hands wrapped around a steaming cup. From the smell, I think it's chai. "You took too long. They'll be awful now."

"Don't fuss, *Amma*." Pari drops a good-morning kiss on her mother's temple. Niharika looks up at her fondly. "They'll be delicious."

"I heard you laughing."

"It's Rachel. She's a ruthless tickle machine."

I blush. It burns hot across my cheeks. Even my ears feel tingly. I fill my plate silently with a couple of the white and golden crepes. There are a few little dishes of chutney, yogurt, and some assorted things at the island. I slide into a seat and dose my plate with a pile of the chutney and a little collection of the other dishes. My restraint has flown, and I tell myself this is a special occasion. My switch has flipped.

Pari gives herself a hefty serving of masala-spiced potatoes. Niharika doesn't have any.

I wonder if that's how she's stayed so skinny despite having Pari and her four siblings. I don't know how she can smell something as delicious as the heady spices in this room and not eat like a mad man.

I break off a piece of dosa and dip it in my chutney. Oh, it's good. Light and fluffy and crispy. "Niharika, this is amazing."

"She means it, *Amma*. You've made her day."

"It's simply breakfast."

I don't answer because I'm too busy stuffing my maw. Oh well. She's smiling at me. I guess kind of fondly? It's better than scowling, and I'm eating yummy things. Whatever works. I'm a charm machine.

Pari and her mom chat for a while. I take a cup of tea from Pari when she gets up to serve herself. It's probably loaded with sugar, but just this once I'm not going to think about it. It's heaven in a cup and goes perfectly with my breakfast.

Pari leans against the island underneath the pale white of a cabinet. She's still wearing the same linen pajamas she had on last night, but now her braid is tousled. I watch her, trying to wrap my head around the fact that I slept in the same bed as this woman. That I woke up holding her hip and with my toes along her calves. Because, oh yes, that sense memory hasn't gone away.

"Does that work for you, Rachel?"

"What?" I jerk myself out of my reverie. I'd been staring at Pari's long, dark hair, wondering how it would feel twisted through my fingers.

"We'll leave around eleven? There are a couple jewelry stores that I think would be our best bet. Then maybe we'll get lunch." Pari sips her tea.

"Um." I glance between Pari and Niharika. They're both looking back at me. No pressure or anything. "Darling. Princess." What *would* I call Pari if she were really mine? "Sweetheart . . . I have to check my accounts. I have a loan payment due on Thursday, and . . ."

She's shaking her head before I can even finish. "I'll cover the rings. It's fine."

I can't help it. I glance at Niharika. She's watching us with a little displeased pinch to her mouth. Pari sees where I'm looking. She comes closer and puts an arm around my shoulder. The soft side of her breast brushes my upper arm. "*Amma*, you should know that Rachel has a lot of accumulated student loans. Close to seventy grand."

I make a choked noise of embarrassment. "Pari," I try to protest.

I told her, but that's not the same thing as wanting it spread everywhere. It's impolite to talk about money. When I was a kid, I wasn't even sure what my mom made, or how much our house cost. Not that I should have known down to the penny or anything like that, but she just always said it was "not my business." In my second year of graduate school, when I finally put together how much my repayment costs were going to be, I wished Mom had been a little more on the up and up.

"*Amma* doesn't care," Pari assures me. She squeezes my shoulders. "She understands."

"Your family didn't help you?" Niharika looks surprised, her eyebrows lifting and her lips parting a little. She puts down her empty teacup.

"Uh, no." I give a tiny little laugh, thinking of Mom offering to pay for anything. She'd worked her way up, and she thought I should have to as well.

Though college costs for her had been a quarter of what I shelled out.

"So Pari, you are supporting Rachel?"

I have a need to defend myself even though, *duh*. That's why we're in this situation. It's why I agreed to marry Pari. Quid pro quo and all that. This is a mutually beneficial situation. But I still don't want to seem like a deadbeat. "I pay for things. Including my loans."

Niharika nods and gives Pari a look that I'm pretty sure says, *We'll talk about this later, young lady.* But they let it go. For now.

# chapter

# *Ten*

*I* still feel terrible by the time we get to the second jewelry store. The first one had been ostentatiously out of anything close to my range. We might as well have been orbiting Pluto for how comfortable I felt there. We'd moved on quickly, I think because Pari had read me as easily as a *Jezebel* post.

The second is a little better. At least they have a couple cases of those tacky round-charm bracelets, which means they aren't stylistically flawless. I have a chance of affording something. My credit card will cry, but it has a little bit of room on it.

Pari grabs my hand. It could have been innocent—we're palm to palm, but she doesn't lace our fingers together. It feels like a lifeline thrown to me in the middle of an ocean. I hold on for dear life.

"We came to this one for a reason," she tells me quietly. "They have a designer line I think you'll like."

I catch her gaze. Does she really know me well enough to be able to choose jewelry for me? My mom specializes in gift certificates—to places I never go—and no ex-boyfriend had been able to pick anything more special than an electric can opener. The only Christmas I spent in a relationship, he got me an iPod shuffle. I liked it, but he got me the dark gray—obviously just what they'd had sitting on the shelf. I wanted the blue version.

Pari walks me up to a small display of rings under glass. She nudges me to sit on a padded stool. My knees buckle. The row of sapphires along one side are particularly beautiful. Tiny chips of the sky and the ocean wrapped in sparkles.

I'm caught. Mesmerized. There's pretty and then there's *pretty*, and the sparklies that Pari has sat me down in front of count as absolutely fucking *pretty*. "What are these?"

She touches the glass as if she's touching pieces of art. "They're a particular designer's work. She's local. I've met her at some parties, and you made me think of her work."

She waves over the salesman, who's a middle-aged man with a balding head and a tubby midsection. She taps the glass. "I'd like to see that sapphire. Second from the right."

There is such crispness, such authority in her expression. He hops to it immediately, bobbing his head in deference.

His patter seems to be automatic. "It's a natural sapphire, hence the paler color. The center stone is one carat, the cut an emerald."

"What?" My attention is finally snatched from the beautiful thing he's holding toward me.

"The way in which the stone has been cut is called an emerald cut. See the rectangular, somewhat vintage styling?"

I nod. My fingertips are numb with how badly I want to touch this ring. It isn't just the stone itself, which looks like the ocean and the sky in a star. It's the nearly bulky design of the metalwork. It should have seemed awkward or graceless, but it doesn't.

Oh, how it doesn't. It's amazing.

"Try it on," Pari urges me.

I take it, but I hesitate before putting it on my finger. I know Niharika is nearby, probably right behind me, but I don't think about her. Pari takes the ring and holds my left hand as she slips it on my ring finger.

I'm shaking.

I've never owned anything like this before. It fits me like putting a missing piece of bone into place.

Even better, Pari is looking at me and smiling. "It's perfect. It fits you."

I know she doesn't only mean the sizing around my finger. The ring turns me into something more than ordinary. I struggle so hard with liking myself, the way my joints are fit together, the way my skin covers me. The fold of my waist. This ring, this hand . . . I like them when they're together. I lace my hands together. The effect carries over to my other hand.

It's just a ring. A stupid ring made of a piece of rock and metal. I shouldn't be this starry-eyed over a twist of metal.

But I am.

Pari is talking to the salesman. He brings out a similar ring, though this one is set with a deep-green emerald. She tries it on, and it fits, plus it compliments her eyes.

"Perfect," Niharika declares. "Now you take them off. Tonight you'll go on a date and do whatever you like, and at the end of the night you ask each other again."

"What?" I say on a weird bark of laughter. Because I do awkward in such a stellar fashion, I clap my right hand over my left as if I'm hiding my precious from Gollum.

"*Amma*, no." Pari is calm, but she's shaking her head. "She loves it. I'm not going to force her to take it off."

Except that makes it even worse. I don't have any idea how expensive this is. I peek at the tag on the inside. The price isn't too bad. I guess. It wouldn't be that bad if I weren't in debt up to my eyeballs, at least.

Niharika has a stubborn set to her mouth and chin. "You're lucky I'm not insisting on a Tamil version of the engagement ceremony."

Pari's eyes narrow. "If we go out, visiting her family is completely skipped." She's bargaining. Even with her mother, she has a sharp edge that shows exactly why she's in the business world. I wouldn't want to go head-to-head with her. Sometimes I wonder if I'm actually getting to know her, or maybe just the side she wants me to know.

"I won't even try."

I'm not sure what the Tamil engagement involves, and I'm glad that my family won't be involved, but I'm uncomfortable with the idea of a date tonight. Especially because I'm not ever letting go of this ring. Metaphorically, of course. I won't surf with it on.

But is this what being bought feels like? I don't think it is. I don't want it to be true, at least. Yet there's no denying that I'm feeling incredibly more positive on the concept than I would have been yesterday.

"*Amma*, can you give us a moment?" Pari asks.

"I'll go browse. Maybe I'll give your father an idea of what to get me for our anniversary."

The moment we're alone, Pari scoots in next to me on the padded stool. I can tell that she's barely hovering on it, probably through dint of will and one butt cheek, but I don't slide over. I think maybe I'd melt into a puddle if I gave up the support of the chair.

"Are you okay?"

"Not in the least," I answer. Yay honesty, right?

"Tell me what's wrong."

"I don't want to be a horrible person." I clutch her arm. She's soft but has enough force to stand up to me.

"But . . . ?"

"I'm not giving this ring up." I crack then, looking straight at her. Our faces are close. Very near. I can smell cinnamon on her breath. "Please don't make me. I'll pay you back. It'll probably take me about six months shy of forever, but I can do without Starbucks or Netflix."

She brushes a lock of hair behind my ear. Her fingertip just barely grazes me, sending a shiver down my spine. "You can have the ring. No matter what."

"I love it."

"I can tell." She holds my hand so that we can both examine at it. She's still wearing the coordinating ring. Our hands look as if they've been posed. My pale creaminess and her darker brown. The rings bring us together. "It's right for you. I stopped at the first store because it's more expensive. I knew *Amma* would like to go there. But for you . . . I knew we had to come here. I was just hopeful this one hadn't been sold already."

How? How is this happening? I'm not sure I understand. "I'm glad it wasn't."

"Besides, buying rings is one more thing for my paperwork. I'll keep the receipts to show in my immigration interview."

I can understand that kind of answer. I wish I could give her more in return. "My mom won't go for the ceremony thing."

"Because it's foreign?"

"Because it's effort she'd have to expend on my behalf." I'm rubbing the ring with my thumb. It's already absorbed my body heat.

"Going out tonight doesn't have to be a big deal. We can sneak out and sit on the beach for a couple hours and talk about nothing." Her shoulders pull in an apologetic shrug. "It would make her happy. I'm not sure why, but it's worth it if we can get out of a step of the process. Wedding ceremonies can be very convoluted."

I laugh, and it sounds a little hysterical, even to me. I close my eyes. I can still feel her. "Yeah, just one small problem."

"What's that?"

I open my eyes again. She's so close. I could crawl into her. Her thigh is pressed against mine, and I know her exact temperature. "That sounds like my idea of a perfect date."

"That doesn't seem bad to me."

I keep my mouth shut. It's easier this way. I don't want to tell her. I may be drowning.

By that evening, I know it for sure. I stand in front of the mirror in the bathroom, my hands on the cold marble. The ring is still on my finger. I don't often look at myself in mirrors. I've learned to skate by them. If I look too long, I always find things I'm displeased with. I wish my arms had more definition. I wish I didn't have such a rounded stomach. I know now that it's not fat, but I bemoan the shape of my muscles.

Tonight I look.

Tonight I see only the haze in my eyes.

I spend a long time getting dressed. By which I mean I spend a long time standing in front of the portion of the closet that has been carved out for me. Right next to Pari's slick business clothes and sophisticated dresses. I touch the sleeve of her wool coat, marveling at its existence in Southern California. She must keep it for traveling.

In the end, I put on a little sundress, because there's nothing in my clothing that comes close to competing with Pari's. And I've always figured if you can't beat 'em, knock 'em out with your assets. Supershort minidress it is.

The dress has long sleeves but a loose, open neckline that drapes down over one shoulder and shows off the fact I'm not wearing a bra. My skin is bare and just sun-kissed enough to keep me from looking like the walking dead without flirting with death by skin cancer.

I braid my hair so it looks artfully bohemian and drapes down over my free shoulder. I spend forever on my makeup, considering

I end up looking like I don't have any on. But my eyes are wide, my cheekbones a good inch higher than usual, and my mouth looks dewy.

Or maybe that's the way I can't seem to close my lips as I stare slack-jawed in the mirror.

Foolish. Foolish, silly idiot.

Who looks beautiful. I do. I look good. I *like* how I look.

That never happens.

I can't help thinking it has something to do with the woman who's cooling her heels in the living room, waiting on me.

I pick up my clutch and leave the cold safety of the bathroom.

My assumption that Pari would be chilling out in the living room is pretty far from true. She's set up shop at the dining room table with her laptop open and a handful of legal-sized folders next to her. Another instance of wishful thinking on my behalf. I tell myself that it's fine she's doing other stuff. That I didn't want her waiting on me. I'm the girl who moons, not the other way around.

I stand in the doorway and hold my Target-bought clutch in both hands. "Maybe we should smuggle your laptop out in a big purse. Starbucks is open till ten. I can be bought with a skinny mocha. Throw in a bagel, and I'm practically your slave."

She blinks as she looks up at me, clearing out whatever thoughts she was chewing through. "What?"

"You seem busy." And I don't want to be a burden. "It's for show for your mom anyway— Oh crap, where is she?" I glanced over my shoulder, but there's no sight of Niharika around.

"She went to bed." Pari caps the pen she's been using to make notes on a legal pad. "Please don't leave me stuck in piles of work. Rescue me."

I'm no one's hero. No one's rescuer. But I smile and hold out my hands anyway. "Then run away with me."

She grabs me and we pretend that I have to haul her out of her chair. But then she doesn't let go of my hand once she's up. She holds both my arms out to the sides and looks me up and down. "You look . . . amazing."

I wait for the squirm of discomfort that so often comes when someone comments on my appearance. It's like I'm filling in the blanks after what they say. That I look amazing for someone who almost starved herself to death. That I look amazing because I'm skinny.

It never comes. I squeeze her hands. "Why are you single, again?"

"I'm not anymore." She flashes a bright white smile at me. "Not for the next two years."

Well now. That's a thought. It's enough to daze me for a little while, until we're in Pari's car and fifteen minutes down the road already.

I look out my window at the passing traffic. "Where are we going?"

"Do you believe in ghosts, Rachel?"

I slip a glance at her. I can't tell where she's coming from. Is she joking? Does she believe in them? "I've never seen one."

"Are you afraid of them?"

"They're not my top fear, no."

We're sliding through Southern California. Cars surround us, but everything moves in the magic way traffic is supposed to, where I get the feeling everyone is cruising along to their favorite happy-place music.

"What is your biggest fear, then?" Pari asks it all casual-like, as if it's a no-big-deal kind of thing.

So I give her my no-big-deal answer. "Clowns. I've heard it means I'm afraid of pedophiles, which seems like a pretty reasonable thing to be scared of."

"Agreed. It's small, closed-in spaces for me."

"Like little closets or like getting buried alive?"

"Neither sounds like a good time, but thanks for those visuals. I suppose the closet would be better than being buried, as long as there was light."

"No light," I say in my best imitation of Bela Lugosi, which is actually a pretty shitty imitation of Bela Lugosi. I make wiggly-creepy fingers and everything. "And you are locked in."

"You're being mean to me." She captures my wiggly-creepy jazz hands—one of them at least. She does have to keep hold of the steering wheel after all.

She's so soft. Her fingers have no calluses, no hangnails. I wonder what they'd feel like touching every part of me.

I wonder what she'd think of touching me. If she'd like it. If she'd want to.

"We're going to a haunted house," she tells me, "but only if you promise to behave. No locking me in anywhere, or I'll hire a clown for your birthday."

"Do you even know when my birthday is?"

When she lists it off, I'm stunned. And a little guilty feeling, for that matter. I know hers is in September? Toward the second half of the month. And I know she's 29. I just wouldn't be able to rattle it off with such confidence. But then, I kind of don't have her confidence at all.

"I'm sorry. I'll behave. Just no clowns."

"Does that mean you don't want to see the reboot of *It* either?"

"God, no!"

From there, we launch into a pop-culture-centered conversation. It takes up the rest of the drive, and the next thing I know, we're in Beverly Hills and pulling past a ten-foot-tall redwood gate and onto a curving drive that's paved with huge squares of terra cotta with grass springing up between. "What is this? Where are we?"

Pari leans forward and looks up through the windshield. "I promised you a haunted house. I didn't say what it would be haunted by."

I'm wordless as I get out of the car and stand before the beautiful grand old dame.

The house is three stories tall. The walls are white stucco. The roof is layered with the beautiful, glowing curved tiles that Spanish-style buildings revel in. The arch over the deeply polished front door is adorned with a glazed mosaic. Dark woodwork accents each window.

But all these are details. The kind of thing that architectural websites drool over and post carefully lit pictures of.

None of them capture the feel of the place.

I turn in a circle in the middle of the courtyard. If it weren't for Pari's compact coupe, I could truly believe myself transported to Old Hollywood of nearly a hundred years ago. If I blink, I might miss Theda Bara's gauzy scarf trailing behind her as she traipses across the pavers on her way to work at the studios.

It's the ghost of a way of life that's been put away that haunts this place. "Whose is it?"

"Now? It's held by a Korean company I've been working with." Pari stands beside me. "It used to belong to Lillian Bosch."

"I don't know that name."

"Most people don't. She only made three films, all of them silent. But she had the good taste to marry a rich man who also happened to be nice to her, miracle of miracles."

"Can we go inside?"

Pari holds up a small keychain with only two keys dangling from it. "After you."

The inside is just as wonderful as the outside. Maybe more so. Everywhere I turn is loaded with architectural detail and furniture that some would kill for. The floor is made of glossy travertine joined so smoothly that I'd have to get down on all fours and feel for the seams with a fingernail. To the right is a step through an arch and down toward a beautiful parlor. To the left, teak doors soar above us. Directly in front are French doors leading onto a patio that looks unbearably lush, accented with trees and plants.

"Where can I go?"

Pari's standing slightly behind me, and I don't look, but I can still hear her smile in her voice. "Anywhere you like. It really *is* supposed to be haunted, by the way."

"Was she sad? Lillian?"

"I don't know. Her husband died early, in 1939, but at least he'd gotten her through the Depression financially sound. She never had kids, but maybe she didn't want them. She lived here until her death in the eighties."

"And never changed a thing." I breathe in the history.

"It doesn't look like it, no."

I throw open the tall doors to our left and find a study lined with deep shelves. Cozy wing chairs are gathered around one end of the room. I want nothing more than to peer through the collection and choose something, anything, to curl up with and read.

But it's not as if I'm going to pass up the opportunity to crawl all over this house. I find stairs in the corner of the room and dash up them, barely conscious of Pari following me.

Lots of people think of the past as being in black and white, but people in the twenties adored color. Lillian Bosch was one of them, and she apparently loved blues and purples best of all. The walls in the upstairs hallway are papered in an outrageous silver-and-purple art deco fan pattern, and things only get better from there.

Pari is my willing accomplice. She's the one who finds the half-sized door in the middle of a hallway that opens to reveal a cage-style elevator. I toss the lever, and we go up and down twice before using it to come out on the third floor. We fall together laughing, so pleased with ourselves that we're going to pop with it. I take the chance to smell her neck, the soft and sultry scent of her. I pull free and run down the hallway before I get carried away.

She chases me.

There's a balcony off yet another bedroom. I slip through the door and shut it behind me, but Pari is close enough on my tail that it's only moments before the glass opens again. With my hands on the waist-high railing, I turn my face up toward the sky. "You found me."

"Were you trying to hide?" Pari lifts a single eyebrow. "You didn't do very well."

The sky above us is that particular combination of glowing and dark that I've only seen in California. The glow is from the breathing, never-sleeping city. The sky absorbs the city's energy and uses it to keep stars far away. It's like there's a shield keeping us in.

"This place is amazing."

I turn to look over the courtyards. There's one right below us, but there's also a second on a lower level, in a portion of the house that's only two stories tall. The rooms open on a symmetrical loop of stairs that showcase a bubbling fountain as their feature. We're on the highest level, which means that I can see the four chimneys, all styled to look like small towers.

"How did you know I'd like to come here?" I'm high with giddiness, the excitement of magic coursing through my veins.

"I saw you watching *Sunset Boulevard* a week ago."

"And from that you guessed?"

She shrugged. "You were whispering along with every word. I figured that meant something about it appealed to you. Unless you have a crush on William Holden?"

"Audrey Hepburn picked the right brother." When Pari stares at me blankly, I shake my head. "*Sabrina*. It stars Holden and Hepburn and Bogart, and she passes on Holden and chooses older brother Linus, played by Bogart."

Pari grins at me. "If you say so."

"This is the knowledge that my degree buys. It's ridiculous, I know."

"It's not." She gets intense all of a sudden. She grabs my forearm, her fingers burning into me. "You lit up when you were talking about it. Don't discount your knowledge."

"Everyone and their brother who's read a review on the internet think they know how to do a close reading of film." I pull away from Pari and look out over the roofs. "I was such an idiot when I went to school. You're right, I do love black-and-white movies. I do love *Sunset Boulevard*. And I didn't take its message until I got ground up and spit out. Old Hollywood is dead. It's all corporate now, and I didn't have a place. I had an expensive piece of paper and a head full of stupid trivia and seizures as a side effect of my anorexia. My student projects were too 'dreamy' and 'unfocused.' I was docked significantly for never having the guts to submit them to film festivals."

"Did you like them?"

"What?"

"Your films. Your projects. Did you like what you had made?"

I have to think about it for a second. My four little films had been so left behind and neglected that I hardly remember them anymore, not what they were actually like. I only remember everything else that got wrapped around them. How controlled I was. How I lived in a haze of barely being able to think, but knowing that if I ate anything other than kale smoothies, I'd be making a grave error.

The films had been sweet. Two had been silent, as befitting my devotion to that period of film. They'd probably been overly moody and lit in a too-careful example of my obsession, but as I think about them, I smile. I wrap my arms around my stomach. I'm so much softer than I used to be, but I have to acknowledge that I can feel the line of my ribs beneath my fingers.

"I did. They were like fledgling birds. Not ready to be shoved out of the nest."

"Then that's what counts." Pari is standing close to me. I don't know how we drifted so near to each other without me noticing. Her eyes are green fire. I think of the emerald she's wearing. The one that's supposed to mean that we're going to be together forever.

But we're carving our own meaning for the rings, aren't we? Pari is changing me. Am I changing her? I want to believe I am, that she seems a little less cool and contained. I don't know for sure.

I don't know anything except the scent of her skin and the hot breeze of a Southern California summer.

"Not all art is for public consumption." She touches the end of my braid. I can't tell if she's looking at me. Maybe she's just thinking. "Some things that are in this world can be private. Hollywood, the world you so desperately wanted to be part of . . . sometimes they seem to forget that. Privacy is not a sin."

I like that. The films I made were mine. They were part of my struggle to find a place. "I'd have been crushed if they'd been panned."

"Then it was smartest that you didn't submit them." She's looking at my mouth. I can feel it. "The act of creation sounds like catharsis. I don't seem to have much creativity in me. I line up numbers and facts and look for the pattern that makes them whole. It makes moviemaking sound like magic, making something from scratch. It's awe-inspiring."

She means it. She's talking to me in a way that makes me almost think that she's not seeing me. Yet she's talking *about* me with such feeling that I'm almost drifting.

"Show me the ghost?" It's the only way I know to carve out some space for myself. And if I don't get space, I'm going to forget how to breathe.

"I'll take you to the room, but I'm not making any guarantees. All I know is what I've been told."

"Good enough for me." Let's not talk about how I might follow Pari off the edge of the building if she assured me it would be worth it. As I follow her, I rub the edge of the ring that hides against my palm.

Pari leads me down the long hallway to the elevator. Then through two rooms that open onto a patio terrace, then through another set of glass-walled rooms. If I actually lived here, I'd get lost on my way to breakfast. I would only drink once I was in bed, because I'd never find my bed again.

The rooms get smaller as we go on, the windows higher up. This is the working end of the mansion. The invisible servants would have retreated to the safety of their territory in order to brace themselves before the next round of orders.

Pari goes up a set of curved stairs similar to the ones in the study in both depth and narrowness. But these have no accent tiles to enliven them. They're white stucco and brown risers and never the twain shall excite. I trail my fingers over the plaster as I go up, trying to imagine everyone who has touched them before.

Whoever they are, they made it through. Probably with less whining than me too.

The hallway above the stairs is a little narrower than the ones in the main sections of the house, but there's still sizeable room. I'm not worried about Pari's claustrophobia or anything, especially since there are wall sconces at each end.

I count six doorways in the small corridor, and we stop at the fourth.

"One of the maids' rooms," Pari says when she opens the door. "None of these rooms are used any longer."

That explains the dusty smell of disuse in the tiny space. We stand hip to hip in the doorway, looking in as if we're little kids who've dared each other to come this far, but can't manage to go farther. I like having Pari's calm breathing to reassure me. We twine our arms together.

There's one bed in the very small room and a dresser at the near wall. A tiny shelf stands bare. There's a row of pegs across from the bed. I can fill in the blanks all too well, though. The pegs would hold the maid's best and second-best dresses whenever she was obligated to be in her black-and-white uniform. Perhaps she'd keep her Bible on the shelf. Maybe she'd have a prize from the carnival next to it, from the time she went with a beau. In the thirties, she might have been relieved to have employment and lodgings, but that wouldn't make the day-to-day drudgery of her work any easier. She'd have looked forward to running away to the movies.

"Why is there supposedly a ghost here? The house is huge, and this room doesn't feel any freakier than the rest."

Pari leans against the doorjamb. "The usual reason. There's a nasty, gossipy story that starts in this room and ends in the fountain upstairs."

"The one on the other roof?"

"Yes."

I want to be there, suddenly. So I leave the small, heartbreakingly normal room behind and make my way to the fountain's burbling peace. Except it doesn't feel as peaceful as it looked from far away. It feels like a reckless place. Like fortunes have been found and lost here. It's off the music room. Even now, a forgotten violin waits on a stand for a player that will never come.

"I assume it was the usual story?" I wiggle my toes free from my heels and stand barefoot on the edge of the fountain. "The maid either loved or rebuffed a man who decided to use his power to hurt her. She was ruined and distraught and killed herself here?"

"You're partially correct." Pari takes off her shoes more carefully, slipping them off one by one and lining them up neatly next to the small pile I'd made of mine. But then she stands beside me. "The maid loved a man, a frequent visitor of the estate. For a while, he seemed to love her in return. But then he turned cruel."

"Don't they always in stories like these?" I could see it unfolding. The maid's perfect curls beneath the peak of her cap. The man would be a financier. He'd have dark hair slicked back from his temples, and he'd look like a god in a tux with tails.

"She let the little cruelties pass, because she believed that he loved her as she loved him. Until she became pregnant. Then she told him no more, that they should 'be as one' and marry for the sake of their child."

"I imagine he didn't run out and buy a ring?"

"Oh, but he did. Lillian was thrilled for the maid she'd always been fond of. She let them honeymoon in that room." Pari points across the terrace at a freestanding suite with its own tall teak door. "The first night, everything seemed fine."

I shiver. Pari is a born storyteller, no matter what she said about not being creative, pausing long enough for me to feel the claws of tension up my back.

"It was the second night that he beat her. Beat the baby out of her, according to medical reports. He concentrated almost entirely on her abdomen."

"Bastard." It seemed an extra cruelty to have married her. To have given her hope that everything would be fine and that her life could begin anew, free of working in service.

"The maid went to the hospital nearby."

"I hope Lillian kicked him out on his ear."

Pari shook her head. She dipped a toe in the clear water. "She didn't. She told the man he could stay as long as he wanted, since she was so sure that he must be upset over his wife's poor health. He stayed another night. The maid died in the hospital that day."

"How sad."

"The man was dead by morning." Pari strolls to the far side of the fountain, in front of the door to the music room. There's a black section of tile there, as if a pie wedge has been sliced out. "Kneeling here, his hands clasped in prayer. But he was dead. Shot. The LA coroner said it was suicide."

"It wasn't, though," I say with a grim sense of satisfaction.

"It's said Lillian did it herself and then danced in the fountain afterwards." Pari looks up at me from under her thick, raven lashes. "But maybe that part's just a story, like the ghost."

I scoop up the hem of my already-short skirt. My entire legs are bare to the warm breeze. I hop into the water energetically enough that it splashes me too. The water is surprisingly warm. Being only deep enough to go to my knees probably means it held the day's sunshine. "It's true. Wouldn't you dance? If you'd taken revenge on someone who hurt your friend? Someone you cared about?"

I twirl through the water, holding my skirts as if for an old-fashioned waltz. I hum as I dance, something old and fancy sounding.

"It would depend on who it was," Pari says from the edge of the fountain.

"Come in. The water's warm."

"My dress is longer than yours. I'd get it wet."

"Then take it off."

I snatch the very air away with my dare. I can't believe I threw the challenge out there. I nearly gape at myself, though I'm looking at Pari. The throbbing beat of my pulse threatens to swamp the water I stand in.

Maybe she'll pass it off as a joke. I've seen her in a bikini, after all. This wouldn't be anything different.

Except, of course it would be.

We both know it, and we don't have to speak a word. The fountain seems to speak for us, burbling into the air in an eternal declaration. I wonder if it has ever been turned off. If it felt given up on after the lady of the house was gone.

Pari takes my dare.

She slides down the zipper that starts under her arm. Her gaze never leaves me, but she can't seem to manage to stay locked on my eyes. She looks at my hair, my legs, all of me. I try not to notice. I don't want to become aware of my body. Not when there's something sparkling and new coming my way.

She unveils herself with a strangely balanced calm and tension. She would delve into me given the slightest hint of welcome. But more than that, she knows who she is.

With a coil of her shoulders, she wriggles free of her dress. It catches first on her sublime bosom before she peels it down to her waist. She wears a creation of lace and satin that looks like some sort of cross between a bra and a short corset. It lifts her breasts like gifts.

She twists the silk of her dress past her waist and hips in one motion, and then she's bending over as she steps out of it, so I can't quite get the whole picture of her. Pari turns away to toss her clothes toward a teak bench. Full silk panties cover and cup a generous ass. The center seam is ruched to make her round globes seem even perkier.

She looks back over her shoulder and catches me ogling her bum.

I pretend like I'm not embarrassed. "I wish my ass looked like yours."

She turns slowly, knowing that I'm taking in every inch of her like a starving woman. I haven't felt true hunger in so long, I almost don't understand its reappearance. Her waist is beautiful. Her hips swell out solely to display that tiny waist and the magic in its rich shaping.

"I don't think that's true."

It takes me a minute to remember what she's talking about. I've been gobsmacked by the perfection of her hourglass. Oh. Yes. That I wished my ass looked like hers. That I wished I had all of her. That I want to live inside her skin.

But she's right, in a way. On her, I can see the beauty of her lushness. On me, I'd be ashamed. I'd see the inches of each thigh like a demonstration of my lack of control. Pari's stomach is soft and gentle, and I want to lay my head on her bare flesh and feel her breaths with mine. On me, that stomach would be gross.

I'm shaking. I'm not as well as I thought I was. I want to hold her. I want to be held. I don't know how to ask for either.

Pari sees me. She sees my need and my dilemma. She comes close enough that she can toy with the feathery end of my braid. I'm still clothed, though my dress barely covers more of me than her undergarments do. Despite that, she's the stronger one of us.

With a single finger, she traces the inside of my wrist and all the way up to my elbow. I watch the movement, silently begging her to stop. Silently begging her to go farther. To touch me in more places.

She doesn't. She reverses her course, trailing her fingernail down the inside of my forearm. "Do you have any tattoos, Rachel?"

"None. Didn't you see on the beach?"

"I was trying to be respectful. I couldn't look at you as much as I wanted to." She toys with the hem of my skirt. It's practically the same as touching my thighs when the thin material transfers the sensation. "I think you should show me now."

I don't want to be naked. I don't want to be seen undressed by anyone, much less Pari. "I think you should kiss me."

Her mouth curves into one of the most beautiful smiles I've ever seen. The white hint of her teeth between her pretty, dark-pink lips is so lovely. "Now? When we're both sober?"

I swallow past the tightness in my throat, but it doesn't do anything to help the tightness between my legs. It's not just my thighs. It's my pussy squeezing itself into something new. "Please. I want to try again."

"Is that what I am, Rachel? An experiment?" There's snap to her words, bite. I try not to flinch. "If that's it, I've been here before. I don't want to do it again."

She might be a lifeline. She might be something more than that. I don't know, and I refuse to think about all the possibilities, so I lean forward and put my lips to hers.

It's what I've done with boyfriends before, and it's always been enough. Given that hint, they have always taken over from there, like marauders who've found a chink in armor. Then I only have to hang on for the ride and let them do what they want.

Not Pari. She's different.

She's patient.

Her lips are soft and bigger than mine. Our mouths are both dry. Our skin more tender than I would have thought possible. Her eyes flutter shut, but I keep mine open. I want to see the individual hairs of her dark lashes. I want to know how the knot between her brows loosens as she sighs into my mouth.

So I kiss her harder. I push her lips apart with mine. I take her breath. We're sweetness, and sweetness turning into ruthlessness. The tips of my breasts tighten to the point of pain. Goose bumps wash across her flesh, and I love it. I love that she's vulnerable for me.

Her hands find home at my hips. Her thumbs cast circles over my skin, the thin material only a ghost between us. I hold her face between both my palms and bury my fingers in her heavy hair. It's too thick for me to find her scalp. Lacework set to trap me. And Christ, but I don't care at all.

I could be caught in her web for a thousand years, and it wouldn't be enough.

We breathe together as one, lean in and then out again. We're something new. I hardly know the fountain water that slips around our knees. It only matters when I try to squeeze closer to her and can't find safe footing. I think I make a sad, impatient little noise.

Pari pulls away. Her grip on my hips tightens when I try to seek her mouth.

"But, please," I whisper.

She sets a finger on my lips. I dart my tongue out and lick her. She hisses a breath. Her breathing comes fast and hard, which makes me realize mine is too. Good. That's what's supposed to happen. This is how we're supposed to be.

"This isn't smart," Pari warns me. Her voice shakes though.

"I don't care." I'd follow these feelings into a lava crater. They feel like they'd immolate me all on their own, after all. Why not let nature do the job as well?

"We have at least two years together."

"Let's make it better."

She pulls far enough away that cold air spills between us. I want to trace the bottom hem of her corselet. It's a track over her skin that marks her curves like a railroad marks a mountain's highest peaks.

"This is a mistake."

She means it. Oh God. This isn't just some "we should, but we shouldn't" sort of foreplay. I curl my hands in on themselves. They feel twice as empty for lack of touching her. My stomach flips. I turn half-away.

I'm not right for her. Of course. That's why she'd thought it would be fine to enter this facade together, that we play at being married. "Oh. Okay."

"Rachel, are you okay?" She touches my shoulder.

I'm cold, I realize. With the sun down, the water can't hold the heat forever. I step out of the fountain, one foot in the black section and one on the orange, Spanish-style. I take a fast, deep breath before looking at Pari. "Fine, honey. Just fine. You're totally right. We have a bargain. Screwing it up would be a stupid mess."

She holds her palms out to me, helpless. I like looking down on her. She doesn't seem so calm, so collected now. I want to tousle her up. "We're getting married in a month, and then I can submit my paperwork. If we have a relationship and it goes south but in less than two years, and DHS is already involved . . ."

"Who says it's going to go south?"

"You've never even been with a woman before." Her throat works as she swallows. "I . . . can't bear it again."

"Taneisha?"

She nods. "She was married to a right bastard. I helped her when she left him. We were friends. While they were separated, she and I became more. And then when she was bored, she went back to her husband."

I don't want to hurt her. Just like I know she doesn't want to hurt me. "A mess. You're right. So you might want to get dressed."

I make myself nod, and it's almost scary how easily the smile comes in its wake.

She hesitates a moment, looking up at me with her green eyes so wide they catch twinkles of light from the music room. But then she steps out of the pool and scoops up her dress. To put it on, she pulls it over her head. Stepping out of it must have been an act for me. "It's *Amma*'s fault. She's the one who insisted we go out on a date."

"I'll make myself scarce over the next few weeks, while you guys get things ready." I hop down. I'm not crying. I'm not shaky. I don't even feel the lust anymore. I've packed it all away into a little cube that I don't want to look at. "I'll be like a real groom. Leave all the decisions up to you."

"Are you sure?" She sweeps the ends of her thick hair out of her neckline before zipping up. "Is that okay with you?"

"I'll go dress shopping." There's no way I'm giving up control of my personal appearance to someone else. They wouldn't know how I need certain cuts that hide the softness of my midsection and cap sleeves to conceal the pudge of my inside arm. "Everything else, we'll let your mom lead. It's fine. It'll make her happy. You'll have lots of paperwork and documentation for immigration."

And maybe, just maybe, it won't make me miserable.

# Eleven

It's surprisingly easy to avoid Pari, despite living in the same apartment. Even when we're sharing the same bed. Pari gets up early with her mom. I sleep in—or I at least try to—and ignore the mouthwatering scents that waft from the kitchen. Denial, my old friend, is back. But I rationalize that it isn't as if I'm denying myself food in general. I eat. I sweep up handfuls of fruit to take to work with me, or I stop at diners and have eggs. I just don't eat in the kitchen. That isn't a warning sign, I tell myself.

It's surprisingly easy to sleep in Pari's bed. She's always asleep by the time I get in, or still working to make up the time that she's putting in with her mom. I brush my teeth and slip into the bed as if it's a hotel bed. I'm happy it's clean and soft. We don't wake up piled on top of each other anymore.

I'm great at compartmentalizing things. It's a gift. Or maybe a curse. I don't know, but it serves me well.

I make nice with Niharika every time I see her. It's here that Pari catches me, in the living room with her mother. Niharika has the TV muted, and she's talking to me about the wedding plans.

I let it go in one ear and out the other. This is none of my concern. This is what makes Niharika happy, and in turn, Pari. That's fine.

That's all fine.

Pari is beautiful. She comes out of the kitchen wiping her hands on a dishcloth. I wonder what she's cooking. Maybe if there are leftovers, I can sneak a little and take a Tupperware to work tomorrow.

"Tomorrow evening is wedding-dress shopping," Niharika tells me. She pats my hand. "You'll come for that, yes? I know Pari tells me you're busy clearing up a big project before the wedding so you'll have time off for the honeymoon, but there's certain things we cannot do without you."

My hand clenches on the back of the couch. "I don't know. Tomorrow?" I'm buying time as I try to figure out what I'm doing. I can't not be involved in buying a dress I have to wear in front of that many people. I bite my lip.

"I'm sure Julian will understand," Pari supplies.

Julian is my boss, and the supposed project I've been pouring my time into is his. But it's not as big a deal as Pari seems to be making it to Niharika. It's Richard's twenty-minute short film, the one he's using to get back on his feet after cleaning up his heroin habit. I'm only supposed to be your average girl Friday on the project. But Julian is out of patience with the guy, so he's putting in the minimum possible effort. I can't blame him. I've added a few lines here and there, maybe cleaned up a character's motivation, and Richard isn't accepting changes easily.

But I have a lot of time on my hands. Patience has made him easier to deal with. Turns out—how surprising—that a man who used to be ridiculously famous loves having someone listen to him for hours and hours.

"We made the appointment as late as we could manage," Niharika says. "Four o'clock."

I swallow the helium balloon that seems to be pushing out my lungs. "I'll be there."

Then I run away. I stay at work, rewriting the script for the fifth time because Richard wants to be able to emote more. I get some sushi and sit in a booth alone, reading on my Kindle. Then I go to the gym. I spend close to three hours between the treadmill, elliptical, and weight machines. By the time I shower, it's late enough that I go home to a nearly dark apartment.

Pari left the light on over the stove for me, and it's just bright enough to get me through the apartment. I slip my shoes off at the door to walk silently. I drop my gym bag on the couch.

Pari is asleep in the huge bed. She's wearing a silken pajama tank top. She clings to the edge of the bed, literally, with one hand wrapped around the corner of the mattress. The other is shoved under her pillow.

I can't believe I made that much of an idiot of myself at the fountain. I shouldn't have started anything. We'd been having a great night until I took it too far.

I want to wake her up and apologize, but that seems even stupider. I'm not sure how I'd string together the words of an apology. It wasn't as if she's been reluctant to put her tongue in my mouth.

Maybe that was the real reason why she pulled away. She's fine with me as a sexual creature. It's fitting me into her life that's more difficult. She doesn't trust me.

By dawn, when Pari crawls out of bed and shuts the bathroom door behind her with a quiet *snick* of the latch, I've talked myself out of apologizing.

Life is easier if you just blast full steam ahead. Plus she doesn't seem the least bit disturbed by our return to distance.

I'm only hurting myself. Like a toddler allowed to scream herself hoarse. Great. Just great. It's like the smack-dab combining of all my issues: a craving to be noticed and an abhorrence of feeling superfluous.

I still keep my eyes smashed shut when she comes out of the bathroom. It's only when she passes me and stands before her dresser that I open my eyes, and then only a slit. She's wearing panties that are full coverage but made of incredibly thin material in a tan color that's five or six shades lighter than her beautiful dark skin.

She tosses her hair back over her shoulder and drops a slip over her head.

I slam my eyes shut before she turns. I keep my breathing soft and just a bit snuffly. With my eyes closed, the pieces of me are invisible. I don't know where I end and the dark begins.

Pari walks by me slowly. I think she touches my shoulder, but it's so light I can hardly be sure. I know that she skims a lock of my hair through two fingers, though. The tug at my scalp is a quiet kiss.

I should open my eyes. I should reach for her bare thigh, waiting right in front of my face.

I don't. If she pulls away again, the sadness will reach inside me and wrench apart pieces.

"Friends" is good enough. Friendship is all I know how to offer, anyway. I'm too needy and broken to be worth all the rest. It's best if I keep my distance.

So I tell myself as Pari disappears back into the bathroom and the attached dressing room. When she emerges, she's flawlessly dressed in a sheath with Jackie O. styling. She's even swept her hair into a heavy chignon at her neck. All she needs is a pillbox hat, and she'd be a million miles above me.

As opposed to the few hundred thousand miles she's above me now.

I decide I'll be cutesy for tonight, for meeting her and her mother at the dress shop, since there's no way I could compete in class. I'll find something simple and as flattering as possible, and I'll be friendly, and that's all we'll need. We'll put my embarrassing little tantrum behind us.

Pari is right. We don't need anything messy between us. If I'm starting to experience something similar to lust, it's probably just a later phase in my recovery, and if I'm patient, I'll start to feel it with someone else.

I hope.

# Twelve

I leave work at noon and go to the gym. I only do an hour on the treadmill. I mostly use the gym for the shower. I blow-dry my hair. I used to wear it even longer than my shoulders, but my illness caused massive breakage. That's what happens when you only give your body a fraction of the nutrients it needs. It's grown a lot since I've entered recovery though. I think I'm going to let it keep growing as far as I can manage. A symbol of my health.

I wear it down around my shoulders. My outfit is carefully picked out: shorts that are probably shorter than they need to be and a nautical, striped top with a boatneck that shows off how I've skipped a bra. I am every inch the California surfer girl. My uniform is my armor.

By the time I pull up to the bridal salon, I almost believe myself.

Niharika and Pari are in a dressing room that hardly seems like it will be big enough for all of us and piles of tulle. Pari wears a white satin robe, and if she isn't naked beneath it, she's at least really damn close. As she sits in a little cushioned chair, she crosses her legs. The robe slides open to reveal a thigh that is soft in both skin and shape.

I smile, and Pari smiles, and I hope that maybe she already knows how silly I feel about my behavior and pouting over the last week. Niharika kisses my cheek and gives me a hug.

"So prompt," she says. "In this traffic, that's a talent."

"I've just learned to leave plenty of time and hide nearby if I get there too early." She thinks I'm kidding. I'm not. This time I only spent ten minutes in my car, sending all my Sims off to work.

"Is your mother on her way?"

I glance between Niharika and Pari. "She's not coming."

"Why not?"

It's such a blunt question. I squirm. "All this has been kind of short notice. She had a commitment she . . . couldn't get out of." My stomach squeezes. I can tell Niharika isn't buying it. The truth is, I didn't ask my mom to be here. When you find the perfect wedding dress, you're supposed to cry, and your mom is supposed to cry too. I couldn't bear to have Mom give it a score out of ten and hear her analyze the cost of the material versus the cost of the dress.

"*Amma*, leave her be." Pari is my knight in shining armor. Or in a dressing gown, at any rate. "Which of these dresses do you like best? Which should I try on first?"

She's distracting her mom for me, I can tell. I throw her my best appreciative smile. Once she has Niharika eyeball-deep in lace, she slides over to me. "There's champagne if you want."

I shake off the calories with a fast no. "I didn't eat lunch. I wouldn't be able to drive home."

"Then how do you want to do this? I have the room next door reserved as well, if you like. But I thought it would be faster if we're together."

I steel myself. This is just a dress. "Together is totally fine."

Pari is happy with my answer. I'm not exactly sure why, but her shoulders seem a little looser.

"Are you looking for anything in particular?"

"Whatever makes her happy." Pari jerks her head toward her mom. "She's been dreaming of this day longer than I have. How about you?"

I shrug. "Not exactly? I want to look good. But I'm not the type who's plotted and planned for my wedding day."

It's part of how I can do this without feeling particularly freaked out about the whole idea. Marriage as an institution is fine, though it seems like there could be room for improvement. But I'd never imagined giving up enough of myself and my life to make it the right thing to do. Maybe this kind of halfway marriage is perfect for me.

I hold the hem of my shirt. "Is your mom going to be okay if I strip? I'm not wearing much but panties under here."

I'm mean. I'm a tease. Because I adore the heat that flares in Pari's eyes. She doesn't take her gaze off me as she calls to her mom. "*Amma*, Rachel is going to get ready to try dresses on. She's not dressed, so don't turn around."

Niharika waves a hand. She's on her knees, inspecting beautiful crystals on the hem of a dress. "*Amaam*, it's fine. No lusting though! You have time for that later. Do you think this could be redone in red?"

"Anything can happen if I pay enough money," Pari answers, but she's still not looking away from me.

I pull my loose blouse over my head. So much for my resolution to behave. She's breaking that no-lusting rule too. Without a word, without a touch, I know she is.

I'm breathing in a way that's different. As if even the air in my lungs knows it's wanted. She's hungry for me.

I know it's the wrong thing to do, but if she's going to be good and I'm going to be nice and make friends again, I still want to know that I can make her burn.

I *need* to know it.

I don't want to look at that part of myself too closely. It might break open other boxes that I'm not ready for.

Instead I grab the robe that's waiting for me on the back of the door. I put it on before I shuck off my shorts, and then I tie it firmly shut.

"How cute," I say, rubbing the pink *Mrs.* embroidered on the lapel. "I have one too."

"I see that." We're grinning at each other like foolish little girls. If this were real, this is a moment where we'd kiss.

I'm relieved when the door opens. We get two salespeople. One is a blonde, the other a Latina with such a wide, friendly smile that I secretly hope she'll be my assistant. I get the short blonde who introduces herself as Nicole, though. She seems nice enough, and when I don't have the magazine pages or internet printouts she seems to expect, she asks me a few questions about my personal style.

I come up blank when she gets to questions about the venue, though. "Pari, sweetheart? Tell her about where we're getting married?"

"We've rented the San Sebastian Wave Club. Decorations are classic with lots of influence from my homeland."

Both salesgirls nod. "I think we have just the thing," Nicole says. She turns to me. "You're about a six? I only ask because your party is on a short timeline, and it's easiest if you can fit in a sample."

I flinch. Jesus. No one's asked me that so flat out in . . . in forever. Not since I was sick, at the very least, and then it wasn't done with much admiration. It was stunned shock at how small I could be and still fit in clothes for grown women.

"Probably." Maybe. Do I want to be a six? I used to be a zero. I thought I'd only gotten up to a four, but maybe I was buying tag-friendly clothing.

Oh, fucking hell. I try to breathe as if this doesn't bother me. I think it's messing me up that I even *am* messed up. I want to be better than this, more healthy. But apparently I'm not if a simple question can send me into a tailspin.

Pari puts a single, calm hand at the center of my back. She says nothing. I don't need her to. My nerves surge with enough intensity that I let it carry me away. I fold inward, the better to know each fingertip of pressure along my spine.

"And red," Niharika adds. "We must have red. It's for fertility."

Pari rolls her eyes, but only facing me, where her mother can't see it. "We're two women. Fertility is going to be difficult."

"You have *double* the fertility." She nods decisively, as if this is how she's come to grips with the concept of her daughter, the lesbian. "It's good luck."

Pari's smile is so warm. It's what I first noticed about her. "Of course, *Amma*. There will be red."

"We have plenty of Indian customers," the Latina says. Claudia is a little bit older and seems steadier. I still wish I'd gotten her as my primary helper. "I think you'll be pleased with our selection."

Three hours later, Niharika isn't anywhere near pleased. I've tried on a couple of dresses, but once it became clear that the real drama was between Pari and her mother, I backed off. I've been sitting on a chaise longue with my ankles tucked under my butt for the past hour. No one's even noticing me anymore, and that's fine.

Pari has had on somewhere close to twenty gowns. Personally, I like her figure in the mermaid style, which shows off her narrow waist and clings to her ripe hips. Her mother has declared that too overtly sexual. Which, come to think of it, might be what I like. But Niharika hasn't liked the princess dresses either, with their wide skirts and narrow, high cut bodices. Nor does she like the sheathe dresses or the A-lines.

It all leaves her and Pari both faintly exasperated.

Pari stands on the small dais in front of three mirrors. The full skirt of the princess style, complete with pickups that remind me of Belle from *Beauty and the Beast*, turns a little more slowly than she does, creating a *whoosh* of satin. She lifts her arms. "Please take this off me."

Both attendants hustle to her side. They strip the clips that have been adjusting the fit of the back and unlace her in moments. She steps down and wraps the robe around her shoulders before sitting next to her mother.

"*Amma*, would you rather see me in a sari?"

Niharika covers her face with her hands. "Am I that obvious? I promised myself that I wouldn't push my choices on you. I'm trying so hard."

"I know you are." Pari curls an arm around her mother's shoulders and gives her a one-armed hug. She probably doesn't realize how it's her father's gesture from when I saw them on Skype. "And you're doing very well. You haven't asked for the coconut ceremony even once."

I think my confusion must show, because Pari shakes her head at me and pulls a face. "I'll wear one. They're beautiful, and it would make you happy. It's the least I can do considering how quickly you've come around, *Amma*."

I don't want to cry, because it's their moment. But man, am I a little jealous too. I have to look away as they hug and Niharika laughs with joy.

"Maybe I can try a few more dresses?" I'm not especially wound up about trying dresses on, but what I intend to offer is a respite. A sort of time-out for the two of them. I don't know how they can be that emotional without burning up. "A little red at the hem might be enough for mine?"

Niharika claps. "Oh yes. That's a wonderful idea. A touch is just right for you. We wouldn't want you to abandon your culture either." She's so sweet. I turn to Nicole. "Can I try the next two?"

The first she brings me is a full ball gown with a plunging neckline that I feel shows off the soft inside of my armpits. I don't like it. I feel stupid for not liking it. I know there are women everywhere who'd be pleased with this dress and looking like I do in it.

"It's not right for you," Niharika says.

Pari stands beside the dais. She strokes the full skirt. "This is too heavy for you. You need something as light and airy as you are."

"I'm airy?" I like that. I don't feel airy from the inside. I feel lost and unfocused. Airy makes me sound like a magical sprite. I'll take it.

Pari hums in agreement, then steps away to talk to Claudia. When she comes back, the dress that's draped over her arms looks like barely more than a column of netting. It's like she's carrying a cloud.

I lift my arms and the two assistants pull it over me. The straps are so skinny; I've had bra straps that were wider. The bodice skims over my torso, overlaid with the netting that makes up a narrow skirt and then pools out into a small train.

I'm mesmerized by the me in the mirror. She's beautiful. With her hair down over her shoulders and her fit body accentuated by the delicate dress, she's the epitome of a beautiful bride.

She's me. I'm her.

I'm not gross. I'm not hiding the unpleasant parts of me. I'm more than the sum of a couple parts that I don't like. I forget the running tally of everything I've eaten for the past five days.

I'm beautiful.

The tears start instantly. I fist my hand in the light silk of the skirt. Niharika is crying too. I hear her sniffling behind me.

Even Pari's eyes are filled with a soft glow. Her smile wobbles. Her hand sneaks into mine, breaking my tight-fisted grip. The only thing softer than her fingers is the inside of my squishy, emotional chest.

I'm laughing and crying all at once. I throw myself into Pari's arms and let my head rest on her shoulder. She holds me while I freak out. It's safe here in the shelter of her arms. I feel a soft brush of her lips over the top of my head. I cry a little more, things that aren't related to the dress at all. I cry for the fact that I'm there without my mother. It's like poison has been lanced from my veins.

The whole time, Pari soothes me. She strokes the length of my back, which is nearly all bare from the wedding dress. Her fingertips tangle in the ends of my hair at my shoulders.

I want more than that, but I can settle for it. I lift my lips to Pari's ear. She smells like expensive perfume. "I'm sorry," I whisper.

"For what?"

"The last week. You're right. We don't need to mess anything up."

"Two years is a long time. We need to stay friends."

Except the very act of how quietly we're whispering and how near we hold our faces is almost too much for me. I don't have deep connections with many people. At this point, it's pretty much only Nikki. But I swallow my feelings the way I swallow everything else.

"Friends," I agree.

She kisses my cheek like a friend would. I hold tight to that feeling. This will be enough for me. I should count myself as happy that I have another friend in this world.

Pari probably has women throwing themselves at her, anyway. I don't want to compete with that. It's safer to be her friend.

Safer for my emotions, that is.

# chapter

# Thirteen

We stop for dinner at an amazing vegan restaurant that's only a block away from the beach. There's a tailor above it and a reiki therapy center next door. The restaurant itself is only a walk-up window with an abbreviated menu above. The seats are all outdoors with mosaic-topped tables.

"What's good?" Pari asks.

"I like the barbecue tofu sandwich. Oh, and the red burrito. Or the black-bean burger with mashed potatoes."

"You like a lot of food," Niharika says. Her tone is approving, but I blush anyway. I do like a lot of food; that's part of my problem.

Pari skillfully deflects. "I think I'm going to get the best of both. The barbecue veggie burger."

"Try the chips," I order her. "They're made on site."

"Yes, ma'am."

I have too many opinions about food. I order myself a tofu sandwich, and Niharika opts for avocado quesadillas.

Once we're sitting at a table with the order flag perched on the edge, I realize I'm on pins and needles. I don't trust the détente that Pari and I have. I don't trust that I can keep to it.

"Tell me about work," Niharika probes. She has the subtlety of an elephant after a peanut. "What studio do you work for?"

"There's no chance you'd have heard of it." I fiddle with the paper from my straw. "We do all the vanity projects. Last month, we charged fifteen grand to make a music video for a kid from Miami who thinks he's going to be the next Justin Bieber. Including peeing on things."

"That seems like a lot of money," Niharika says, concerned for a stranger she's never met.

"Trust me, his parents can afford it. They kept trying to shove more money at us. 'Are you sure more backup dancers wouldn't help?' I think they knew how bad their son is but still wanted to make him happy."

"More backup dancers make everything better," Pari says. "I wish I had backup dancers right now."

"Oh yeah? What would you sing about?"

"Love, of course. Aren't all songs about love?"

"Except the ones that are about sex," Niharika adds matter-of-factly.

Pari and I both burst into laughter. I can't speak for Pari, but mine was the combination of elegant and maternal with such frank mention of the dirty stuff.

"What? You girls laugh, but there's a reason Sadashiv and I have been married for almost forty years, and it's not that he likes my dosas. Though he does."

"*Amma*," Pari protests, though I'm not sure what she wants now. The cat was way out of that bag.

I fold my hands and rest my chin on them. "Do tell."

"Do not!"

Niharika wrinkles her nose at her daughter, and Pari is saved by the arrival of our food. It looks so good that I feel the hunger at the bottom of my stomach. I push away the top of the bun to balance on the edge of my plate. No one needs that many carbs at one go. Just to be safe, I dump too much salt on it, so it'll be inedible if I'm tempted to pick at it later. I cut the rest of the sandwich into four pieces. It would be good if I could stop eating at two sections, but if I have three, I won't be too mad at myself. My back would look leaner in the wedding dress if I stayed on the bottom end of my weight spectrum. Then the red-and-gold ribbon that Niharika wants to add won't just point to my squishy lack of muscle tone.

I look up from cutting my fresh kale salad into a more chopped style, because I like it better that way, and Pari is watching my silverware. I catch her gaze and lift my eyebrows, but she only shakes her head.

I know I have a lot of leftover habits from my unhealthy days, but they're just that. Habits. Not the crutch they once were.

"What are you working on most recently?" Niharika looks interested, but I can't tell if she's just making conversation or if she really cares. Maybe a little of both, in that way we all have with people we don't really know yet.

"There's an actor who's paying us for a short film. It's taking most of our effort this month."

"And how are you helping?"

"Me?" I smile and cock my head. "I mostly make the coffee runs."

"I don't think that's true," Pari says as she studies me. She munches a chip.

"Eh, I help a little bit. Julian doesn't like this guy much."

"Who is it?"

"*Amma*, unless he turns out to be Rajesh Khanna, you're not even going to know who he is."

"That's not true," she replies firmly, emphasizing her point with a poke of her plastic fork into her quesadilla. "I know the Chrisses. Hemsworth, Pine, and Pratt Pratt Pratt."

"That is precisely right."

Pari rolls her eyes at me. I pretend I don't know what her problem is. Her mom is adorable.

"You both have to swear to never say a word, okay?" I lean in across the table and whisper the name.

It's actually Pari who has no idea who I'm talking about. Niharika lights up and gestures with her fork. "Yes! I know him. He was in that show with the detective. He had a very fine car."

"Yup, that's him. And then he got a very fine heroin problem. But then he got sober, and he wants to prove he can still act." I take a bite out of my sandwich. It's so good. I'm glad I salted the top half.

"Can he?" Pari has a tiny bit of barbecue sauce at the corner of her mouth. Her pink tongue sweeps out to clean it up, and I completely lose my train of thought.

"Can he what?"

"Act?"

"I guess he's fine. As good as most of them. His problem is he may have lost his charm. He's tired, and the camera can tell."

Pari angles toward me. "What do you mean 'the camera can tell'?"

I smile because I know I'm going to sound ridiculous. "The camera can tell secrets that you don't want the audience to see. The best actors? They're the ones who let truth through. Directing is the art of harnessing another part of reality." I shrug, brushing it off. "At least, that's what I always thought. But no one really seemed to agree with me, so maybe I'm just talking out my ass. Sorry, Niharika, my butt."

She has a mouthful of quesadilla, but she doesn't seem too bothered by my slip anyway.

Pari pushes her food around on her plate. She looks up at me suddenly, and I know that whatever she's going to say is going to leave me . . . different. "Tell me what you've really been doing with this production. We won't tell anyone."

"I don't know what you mean."

"You're not just the coffee girl. And you try to talk of it dismissively, but there's something there. That you're not saying."

Niharika smiles at her daughter. Do they realize they have the same smile? It looks different on the more mature woman, since her cheeks are a little heavier and the skin around her eyes softer. But their truth always shows through. "Listen to your *kadhalan*. She knows you."

Pari and I trade glances. Except that isn't the right word for it. Her gaze traps mine. I'm at her mercy. She does know me. And I think I'm coming to know her . . . but she still doesn't want me.

"I've rewritten it. I'm doing some of the principal photography, but only when Julian is busy with projects that annoy him less. I can't tell anyone because the actor wants to retain screenwriting credit if it does well."

"If it does badly, he'll throw you under the bus," Pari says coldly. "That's the kind of person who wants it kept secret."

I shrug and ball up my trash, which includes about half my food. I shouldn't feel proud of how much I left on my plate. I shouldn't.

I do.

"It doesn't matter. He's not a bad guy. He wants back in the industry is all."

"Is it good work?"

"It's a fuck load better than it was when he gave me the pages." I wince. I hadn't meant to say that.

"Then it's yours. And you deserve credit."

"I'm not taking credit." I push away from the table. I might be running away from the conversation.

Pari doesn't let me go though. She follows with her own trash and shoves it into the recycling and compost compartments after I'm done. "It's your work."

"That's not *where* I work. That's not the kind of work I do. We're not the kind of place that gets that sort of credit." I'm angry. Holy crap, I'm angry about this.

It hardly even makes sense, but I revel in my anger. I haven't been actually furious in a very long time. Now it's Pari who isn't listening to me, who's insisting on something that I can't do. It's not acceptable, and I'm so mad that I could stomp.

I don't, but mostly because my sparkly gold flats wouldn't make a satisfying *thump* on the patio tiles. "It's my business, Pari. My job. You don't get to tell me what to do."

"Why not?" She looks at me head-on. Her hands are by her side and open.

I tried on wedding dresses with this woman an hour ago. I'm going to marry her in two weeks. And I am absolutely, incandescently furious. I luxuriate in my rage. I let it fire my blood. I'm only moments from letting out some primal roar. "Because I'm my own fucking person!"

"Good," she says through locked teeth and what looks a little like a smirk. "Good. Hold that. Feel it. Then go tell your boss to shove it, that you're going to make your own pictures from now on."

"It's not that easy." I'm spitting. I try to let it go, but my fury is something new, and I like new and shiny things. "I don't work at that type of studio. I knew it when I took the job. I went *looking* for it, Pari."

"Why?"

"Because I can't handle the industry for real. I'm not made for it." I freeze. I don't think I've ever said that out loud. Air fizzles out of me in a long, slow breath. I shake my head. "It doesn't matter."

"It matters. You matter."

"I'm not anyone special. I've seen better people than me who're more gifted and more talented not make it."

"You're special to me."

# Fourteen

our little words. They were only four little words. I hold them to me like they're made of gold or maybe glass. Glass, because it's fragile and will shatter if I drop it. I won't ever drop those words. I don't mean to ever let them go. I crumple them up in the deepest part of me and carry them with me for the next few days.

They show themselves at the most surprising moments. When I'm standing in line for coffee. When I'm working on a few pages of the script.

When I'm in minute fifty-three on the elliptical, and then they make me wonder if I should keep going. Maybe I should go home.

I go home more often. Niharika cooks dinner, and Pari lets her. They fill the apartment with laughter.

One evening I unlock the front door to an overwhelming wave of giggles. I hitch my gym bag higher over my shoulder as I head toward the kitchen. They're always in the kitchen. It's their favorite place to hang out, it seems like. Tonight it's filled with the scent of bread. I can smell the carbs in the air.

"Hey," I say at the doorway.

Pari is at the stove, which is the unusual part of the picture. Niharika is sitting at the island. Spread out in front of her is a poster-sized diagram. She has a lined notebook next to her right hand too.

Pari looks at me and smiles. She's tired. I see it in the weariness of her cheeks. "Hey."

I use the pretense of giving her a kiss on the cheek to get closer. "Are you okay?"

"Just tired." She shrugs. She glances back over her shoulder before leaning closer to me. "*Amma* is driving me nuts. We're up to three hundred and fifty guests."

I manage not to gasp.

"I heard that, young lady," Niharika says without ever lifting her head. Her hair is parted down the middle and smoothed into a thick braid that hangs down her back. "We have a large family. We've been blessed."

I like that Pari leaves her hair down so often. Will that become part of her maturity, braiding her hair? I won't know, not in the same way that I get a look inside her life right now. If I'm lucky, we'll be the kind of friends who meet for lunch monthly. Her life will probably be too full for more than that.

Pari gives me a strained smile.

"Is there any way I can help?"

"Dinner will be ready in a few minutes. Come make conversation that doesn't have to do with wedding plans, and I'll love you forever."

"Consider it done. I just have to get showered up." I flick toward my sweaty tank top and yoga pants. "I'll make it fast."

Pari's gaze travels up and down me. I shift from foot to foot. "What?"

"Nothing," she answers, but it has enough bite that it doesn't feel like nothing.

I shrug it off though. She's stressed. I give her another kiss on the cheek, even though I don't want to get closer for fear of rubbing my sweat on her.

I love the shower in the master suite. It's worth the price of admission, no matter what it cost. Two showerheads are mounted on opposite walls, with a waterfall-style one at the ceiling. After I've done the actual work of getting clean, I stand beneath steaming-hot water, letting it turn my skin pink. The sting is so sweet that it's good. I drop my head back until I'm getting water pattering down on my face. With my eyes closed, it's like standing in the rain.

Maybe after the wedding, when Niharika goes home and I have to go back to the other bedroom, I can bargain for time in this shower.

I giggle as I shut off the taps and wrap a bath towel around myself. I look at the countertop for my change of clothes, but the creamy marble has nothing clothes-like on it. I've forgotten them. Damn it. I don't want to take longer than necessary, since Pari needed help, so I tuck the towel tighter under my armpits and hustle into the bedroom.

Where Pari is waiting.

"Oh!" I think I'm blushing, but the water left me so flushed that it's kind of hard to tell. The tips of my ears tingle. "Sorry, did I take too long? Is dinner ready?"

"How long were you at the gym?"

I turn away and pull a pair of panties from the top drawer of my dresser. I step into them and pull them up under the towel. Instantly I feel a little more dressed. Funny how those silly things work.

I laugh. At what, I'm not really sure. "Are you doing the nagging-wife thing already? I don't need you to rescue me. I didn't think we had that kind of setup."

"Were you there two hours?"

"How do you know that? Are you tracking me?"

She shakes her head. "It was a guess."

I turn away from her again and shrug into a bra. I let the towel slip once I'm mostly covered. "I'm not going overboard. Most of my time was in the sauna, relaxing. Julian was an asshole this afternoon. He asked me *yesterday* to interview extras, then got mad at me today because I'd only called three casting directors. If he needed it done faster, he could have just told me."

Pari's shoulders loosen. "He doesn't deserve you."

"You're sweet to say that."

And then. Then. That's the moment I realize that I'm almost naked, and I'm pretty sure it's the moment that Pari realizes it too. Nothing changes and everything does. I actually back up a step, but it's okay because Pari . . . she comes two steps closer.

The air in my lungs is thick. I whisper her name. She doesn't answer.

We collide instead. Our mouths seek each other. Lips to lips. My hands wrap around the sides of Pari's face. She's smooth. Christ, so tender. She buries her fingers in my wet hair. It tangles and sticks, pinching my scalp, and I couldn't give a shit.

Because Pari is kissing me and I'm kissing her.

We push together so hard that I stumble into her. She turns us. We're the same height, and it makes our mouths align perfectly. She tilts her head, tongue sliding across my bottom lip. My breasts are tight, but that's astounding because hers are on me. We're softness to softness.

I find her curves. I touch them all because she might take this away again. Her back is smooth, and her waist sweeps in. I lose my courage when my palms find her ribs and, instead of touching the sides of her breasts, I reverse direction again. I find an opening at the hem of her blouse and shove my hand up her back.

Silk has nothing on her. Satin has nothing. Baby duck fluff has nothing. I have no words to compare with the suppleness of her skin and the gentle give of her flesh. I just try to touch her everywhere I can.

When I get handfuls of her round ass, she makes a sound that's both quiet and hungry at the same time. She takes my lip between her teeth, then licks away the sharp pain she's given me.

My hips are rolling. I only realize it when she holds my waist in one hand and gently pins me to the wall. Cold washes over me, but I run hot with shivers almost immediately when I realize she isn't going anywhere except to take her mouth to my throat.

"We shouldn't be doing this," she says, then opens her mouth on my neck. I'm sure she can feel my throbbing pulse.

"I know." I close my hands tighter on her ass. She grinds her hips into mine. "Two years is a long time."

"We can't break up." She adds in teeth. "Not that we're together."

"But I know what you mean. Where's your mom?"

"Her cousin called and asked if she wanted to go over." Pari finds my breast. With only my lacy bra in the way, it's almost like she has me bare. My back arches into her touch. I let my head fall back against the wall with a *thump*. She pinches my tight, beaded nipple, and *holy shit*, I didn't know I could work that way. What is this magic? Is she just this good? Because it feels like more than I've ever done all wrapped up into one encounter.

When I open my eyes, Pari's watching me too. Not watching her hands on me. Not watching my body. Her gaze is boring into me. She's attuned to me.

"Please," I whisper, because somehow I know that's what she wants to hear. I'm attuned to her too. "Please touch me."

She does one better. Her mouth follows the line of my collarbone and then opens over my shoulder. She bites me, and I jump into her touch. We're electric. I lose track of parts of me and parts of her. We're sliding down the wall, and I don't care at all. I'd do anything to never stop this.

She pulls my hips closer to hers. I lose my balance. We go tumbling down in a pile of limbs twisted together the way I'd always thought sex worked. It isn't the fumbling I've had before. It's still awkward, but in a different way, because we're awkward together.

I end up on the bottom. The softest carpeting in the world is still rough on skin that isn't meant for it. My shoulders sting. I wouldn't stop this for the life of me.

Not when Pari's hand opens over my stomach. I try to suck flat, but she notices and bends to nip the edge of my ribs.

"Give me you," she orders.

I breathe and melt all at once.

Her hand slides under my panties. I've just put them on and they're already soaked. How did I not notice that? She strokes between my labia, and only then do I realize that I'm throbbing there just as hard as my pulse is throbbing. With each touch, I explode. She explores me slowly but so fucking efficiently. It's obvious she's done this before, had her hand down a woman's pants, and later it might bother me, but right now I'm so fucking grateful.

She finds my clit with unerring navigation, finding my opening first and sliding straight up from there. Her fingertips slip and slide around it. I'm encircled. She rubs along both sides at first.

I have my eyes open, and she's leaning over me. Her hair creates a curtain around us. We're divided from the world, separate. Her gaze flickers between my eyes and my mouth. She's taut and focused in the very opposite way of me. I'm floating free, even though she's stretched along my side. She has one leg thrown over both of mine, and I can't tell if it's because she's trying to hold me still or because she wants to get closer to me. Maybe both. Maybe it doesn't matter at all.

I take a while. I always do; it's no reflection on her skills. On the way she devours me. She doesn't seem to mind. She lets me build slow—and when I start to get close, she slows down even more. I get the feeling I could take three days longer than eternity to come and she'd see me through.

And that thought alone is enough to send me spinning over the edge into release. It's one of those lit-fuse orgasms. The ones you can see coming from a mile off, and I have to remind myself to keep breathing because holding my breath in anticipation only makes me dizzy and my ears buzz. Then it's there and it's inevitable, and I gasp great honking chunks of air that almost seem to catch in my throat. It's not a pretty climax, none of those soft moans that signify delicacy. I'm hissing and nearly choking. I can't turn it off.

I don't want to.

Pari doesn't try to shut me down, either. She opens her lips over the tip of my breast. Her mouth dampens the lace, and the combination of scratchy and slick adds an extra layer of sensation to everything. I want to drop away. It's all overwhelming.

Pari gentles me through the final peak as I clench over her fingers. My back bows and grinds my shoulders across the rough nap of the carpet. Pari finally stills, slowing the way she's teasing me, holding the center of my body in a cupped hand. She's soaked, which means I'm soaked, because it all came from me.

I turn my head and try to bury my face in her shoulder. She's still dressed. Her V-neck T-shirt is washed soft, the cotton scented with laundry detergent and the heady spice of whatever she'd been cooking with. I don't think I'm crying. I think that's just the way I'm breathing, still in shaky sobs. Except there's a sting in my nose, and my eyes are leaking just a little bit.

I turn away from her and put my arm over my eyes.

"Look at me," she says.

I should have known that Pari wouldn't let me hide. I take my arm down, but I still can't look at her. I stare up at the ceiling instead. "I guess we have to talk about this?"

Her hand is still curled over my pussy. She pets my underwear back into place. I'm not sure what good they'll do. I'm going to have to change since they're so wet, they're unusable. "We should."

I turn my whole body into her until we're curled forehead to forehead and knees to knees and toes to toes. It makes Pari stop touching my pussy. I'm a little relieved. I don't like knowing that someone else seems to understand my body better than I do. Her hand comes to rest on my hip instead. Her thumb traces patterns in the hollow next to my hip bone. I don't think she realizes what she's doing. I'm afraid of saying anything because she might stop.

"It was good. Really, really good."

Her smile turns smug enough to make me squeeze my knees together again. "I know."

"But it doesn't have to be anything more than that." Liar, liar, liar. But it's safer this way. "We're becoming friends. Right?"

"Right."

"Then we're just really close friends."

"With benefits?"

"Maybe once or twice." I trace the shape of her bottom lip with a fingertip. Her mouth is always full, but right now it seems nearly swollen. From kissing me and sucking on my flesh. The truth of that sends a wicked thrill through me. "I owe you, for one thing."

"You don't. You don't have to do anything you don't want to."

"I want to," I say, and it's more true than any of the other times. Than any of the guys.

When I was sick and desperate, there were a lot of them, and I did want to, but not in the same way I do now. I knew it would make them like me.

This time, I'm not sure that doing for Pari will make her like me at all. If I seem like another woman who's using her for experimentation, it might push her further away. But it would make me happy to have my hands on her body. So I will.

All I have to do is talk her into it.

## Fifteen

"I think she's avoiding me."

"You live together," Nikki replies. "How good can she be at it?"

We're in Belladonna Ink, the tattoo parlor managed by Nikki's girlfriend. Skylar is at her booth, cleaning and preparing for opening later in the day, but at nine in the morning, a tattoo parlor isn't exactly a happening place. It's just the three of us.

I'm lying on a bench in the reception area. It was upcycled from a church pew, except Skylar's business partner reupholstered the cushion with striped, candy-colored fabric. I have my feet on the wood and one arm hanging loosely over the edge. Nikki is sitting on the receptionist's stool.

"Better than you think," I answer her.

She spins as she considers my case. "But you're still sleeping in the same bed?"

I nod, then have to use my words like a grown-up would. "Yeah. But she hangs out with her mom *constantly* unless she's at work. I can't get them apart. I thought about pitching sex as another thing we could chat up at the DHS interview, but maybe that's not a great idea."

"Wake her up with oral sex," Nikki says simply.

Skylar's head comes up. "That's a consent violation."

"You're not supposed to be paying attention to our conversation."

"I can't believe you told her," I say to Nikki.

She has the good grace to look ashamed. "I'm sorry. But she's bae. We're, like, joined."

Skylar snorts a little. "You're ridiculous."

"Love you too," Nikki says before blowing a kiss toward her girlfriend.

I half expect Skylar to ignore Nikki, because the blown kiss is obviously a joke. Skylar is always a badass, but she melts toward her surfer girl and smiles. "Love you too. Bae."

"Does this make me gay? I know this is dumb, but I don't know how I didn't notice, you know? I grew up here." I throw my arms wide. "San Sebastian cares more if you buy organic produce than it does if you're a lesbian."

"Do you think I'm hot?" Nikki asks.

I give it a little consideration. Nikki has very long, very straight brown hair that she perpetually kept up in a ponytail until she met Skylar. Now she wears it down occasionally. She's a professional surfer, so her build is pretty athletic from all the hours she spends in the water. Right now she's wearing shorts that show off her long, tanned legs, and her feet are crossed at the ankles in a pose that's unintentionally pinup-like.

I met Nikki years ago when we were both in middle school. Our bond became unbreakable over our mutual slutty phases. Nikki kind of outgrew it when she realized she was gay, though she used to make regular pilgrimages to dive bars outside town to get laid. She was one of the few friends who kept putting in the effort to keep in touch with me when I was my sickest and trying to cut away the world so I'd be free to go away.

Three days after my graduation from my master's program, she took me for a drive. We stopped at an anonymous building in the middle of downtown Costa Mesa. She'd told me it was a rehab. And that I needed to go.

And yet . . . "Nope."

"How 'bout her?" She points at Skylar.

Skylar looks up from the pieces she's been loading into the autoclave. She's an entirely different type from Nikki. Her hair is very dark, but clipped short around her ears in an asymmetrical boys' cut with edgy stripes razored above her left temple. Today she has on a plain white T-shirt over straight-cut jeans, which is kind of the most feminine outfit I've ever seen her in. And she's covered from the neck down in ink.

"Nope. Sorry."

Skylar tips a wink at me. "No harm done. I'm taken anyway."

"Damn right." Nikki spins again. "Do you ever see anyone, boy or girl, walking down the street and think, 'Gee, I'd like to bone them'?"

"Thanks for that descriptive phrase, but no. I don't." I bounce my knees. "I think my sex drive is defective."

"It's not defective to be demisexual," Skylar offers.

"What?" I sit up. "What is that?"

She stops what she's doing with the autoclave and looks at Nikki. "I thought you were going to talk to her?"

"What?" Nikki's eyes are big, and she throws her hands up. "It's not my job to be her sexual counselor."

"Um, yes, it is." I wish I had something to throw at her. Just like pillow level or something though. I'm annoyed, but not murderous. "It's in the 'best friend' description."

"I missed the description. Was that in a memo?"

"It was carved on the back of the locket I gave you. You know, the one that was half a heart?"

"Didn't happen. You're making things up again."

"Maybe." I look at Skylar instead. "What is a demisexual?"

"It's a descriptor. Like queer or bi, except this one means on the sexual to asexual spectrum. You're somewhere closer to asexual, but not all the way there. Demisexuals usually only want a sexual relationship with someone they already have an emotional connection with."

"That doesn't sound so bad."

"Totally isn't," Nikki says. "And I didn't tell you because it's just a word. You do you, ya know? But it seems like maybe that's you. I mean, I can't remember you ever just locking eyes with anyone and thinking they're droolworthy."

"No, that doesn't sound like me." Part of that's because I start worrying that sex would mean them seeing me at my ickiest, though.

I didn't think that about Pari. I wasn't worried at all. I lie back down on the bench with a sigh. "I don't think that solves my current dilemma though."

"How to get your fiancée to bone you."

I cover my face with my hands. "You don't have to say it like that."

"How to get your fiancée to make sweet, sweet love with you?"

"That sounds even worse."

Nikki grins with self-satisfaction. "I know."

"When's the wedding?" Skylar has a bottle of distilled water in her hand as she fusses around with her cleaning. I wouldn't tell her, but it's kind of amusing how particular she is about her studio when she looks like such a rebel badass.

"One week from today. Which I should fucking hope you two would know, because you're invited. And I have like eighteen people coming, so you *have* to come." I rub my eyes with the base of my palms. "I think Pari has over three hundred. They're all family from what I understand. Or friends of the family. Or friends of friends."

"She knows," Nikki says in assurance. "Well, her phone knows. I marked it off on her calendar, and I'll drag her there."

"I have a suit," Skylar offers. "Looks damn good."

"I have a dress. A white dress. Can you fucking believe it?" I shake my head. If you'd asked me five years ago, this scenario would never, ever have turned up on my list of possibilities. "If I don't figure something out, I'll be going to the altar without ever having slept with my future wife."

"That *was* the original plan." Nikki leans back against the counter. Her feet swing free. "Unless you've forgotten?"

"I haven't forgotten anything. I don't know why it's driving me so damn crazy."

"Coz you got a case of the hot pants for the first time in your life."

"Hot pants?" I laugh. "What's the cure?"

Skylar leaves her tattoo booth and strolls toward her girlfriend. She catches Nikki's face between both her hands. The ink tattooed across her knuckles next to Nikki's delicately tanned, pure complexion looks faintly obscene in a way that makes me squirm. I'm thinking about the way my skin and Pari's skin looks side by side.

It only gets worse when Skylar kisses Nikki deeply. I can see their jaws move, see the way their lips cling. As they separate, Nikki's tongue darts out for one last taste of Skylar, as if she can't bear to be separated.

Skylar's gaze finds me first, from the corner of her eyes. She leans her forehead against Nikki's, and I realize they're both breathing hard. That easily. That quickly. Skylar looks at me, but Nikki is still looking at her. Completely bound up in whatever dirty thing has caught her attention.

"The cure is to find someone who wants in your pants exactly as badly as you want in theirs."

"I don't know if that's Pari." She's closed off from me. I can't get inside her head. Is it about me, or is it about her? Sometimes I can't tell. She's so driven, so perfectly contained.

"Then you need to find out. And if it's not, you two stay friends. Not friends with benefits. Because you'll need time to yourself to go out and start again."

Nikki's hand is at the back of Skylar's neck. She's stroking her girlfriend almost absentmindedly, but the look she turns on me is fierce. "Because you deserve it, Rachel. You deserve someone who wants you just as you are."

***

I leave them before the shop actually opens. Nikki will probably hang out for a while before leaving to catch the afternoon tide. She heads out for a competition in Brazil the day after my wedding, so she has to be prepared.

I go back to the apartment, but it's empty. There's a note on the fridge, scribbled in Pari's writing. *Went to office. Amma is at cousin Sunil's.*

The paper is smooth under my touch, but she wrote firmly enough that I can feel the indent of each letter. She sneaks in work here and there, around Niharika's planning and visiting. She's the best daughter I've ever known. I wouldn't do the same thing for my mom, but I think that's maybe because she trained me that way. Why should I give her what she doesn't give me?

Pari's office is in downtown LA, in the financial district. On weekday mornings, it's a hell of a commute, but it shouldn't be too bad at this hour. It would probably only take me an hour to get there. That would leave me plenty of time to Yelp the best lunch place around and pick up a takeout order.

Impulsively, I change my clothes. I throw on a sundress and pull my hair up into a French braid. I pretend I don't know what I'm doing, because it's easier that way. It's so easy to pretend too. I shove all the other thoughts in a little box. I listen to Lana Del Rey once I'm in my car. Singing along helps me clear it all out even more.

I'm just being nice. I'm just taking lunch to my friend. I'm just, I'm just, I'm just . . .

*I'm just sliding through my life, trying to avoid the fact that I exist.*

The thought hits me like a hard bolt upside the head as I turn into a parking garage less than a block from Pari's office building. By the time I'm pulling into a slot, I've wiped it out of my head again, because I'm good like that. A queen at compartmentalizing.

The Mediterranean bistro I find nearby has great reviews. I place an order for a layered, intricate salad and a combination plate of falafel and roasted veggies. They box it up quickly, and before I know it, I'm standing on the Los Angeles sidewalk, staring up at a skyscraper. The black-glass lobby door is locked. There's a keypad next to the far-right door, but of course I don't know the code. Duh. With all my shoving thoughts into little boxes, I hadn't managed to pick this thought out.

I back up until I'm leaning against a parking meter, and then I pull out my phone. I'm still watching the mirrored glass above me as I dial Pari's cell phone number. "Pick up, pick up," I mutter.

"Hello?"

"What's the code to get into your building?"

"What?"

I hold back a burble of laughter that would be somewhere between hysterical and nervous. This is such a stupid idea. The afternoon sun slants between buildings to lance across my already-hot neck. My fingers are starting to sting like hell where the bag of food is cutting into them. Plus it's probably all getting cold. "I'm outside. Like, on the sidewalk."

"What? Why?"

"Because I brought you lunch?" Even I can hear the weird uplift my voice takes at the end of the sentence. I try again. "I brought you lunch."

Silence hisses on the line for an uncomfortable moment. "From San Sebastian?"

"No, from a place around the corner. So, you know, you could have totally gotten it yourself. But I drove an hour and fifteen minutes for no real reason, just so I can stand on the sidewalk with a homeless guy staring at my legs." I turned slightly away from the crusty old guy with a Vietnam vet ball cap smashed down over his ears sitting one parking meter down. "Please let me in?"

She tells me the floor and buzzes me in. I pass the homeless guy a weak smile that's probably not enough of an apology, because even though he really was looking at my legs with the fascination of a kid at a magic show, that's no reason for me to feel uncomfortable. I don't think.

I'm swept upward by the elevator. As each floor flips by on the display, I get more and more nervous. If Pari isn't happy to see me, I'm not really sure what I'm going to do. Hand her a bag of food and turn right around again? Sounds like the most socially ill-adjusted thing I've ever done in my life. Perfect.

When the doors start to open, my throat is locked tight.

Pari is smiling.

I can breathe.

It's a gentle smile, and her head's tilted curiously. She's wearing designer jeans and a loose silk tunic. Her killer spike-heel orange pumps make the outfit. She looks absolutely stunning. I want to touch her hair, feel it slip through my fingers.

"I brought you food," I offer instead as I hold the bag out.

She takes it, cradling the Styrofoam containers in both hands. "It smells fabulous."

"I hope it's good."

Small talk. As if small talk isn't bad enough, it's awkward too. Lovely.

I follow her down the hall to her door. The carpet is plush, and the walls are studded with dramatic abstract art at regular intervals. She's left her door open, and calming classical music reaches toward us.

It's not a corner office, but the wall of windows is still pretty good. She has space enough for a small sitting area with a love seat and a cushioned chair on one side, and her expansive L-shaped desk on the other side.

I stand in the doorway as she switches off the music, then waves toward the love seat for me. She puts the food down on a low table and goes to her credenza. "Sit, it's fine. I think I have some silverware in here."

"They were supposed to put silverware in there. Well. Plasticware, at least."

The plastic bag rustles as she pokes around in it. I swear to God I can hear the thump of my heartbeat. I wish she hadn't turned off the music.

"Yes, here we go," she says, and triumphantly waves a white fork.

It's like being in middle school and trying to make friends all over again. I wish the ground would crack open and swallow me. It'd be a long fall from this many stories up, but totally worth it.

Pari opens both take-out cartons and lays them on the table between us. "This looks great."

"I wasn't sure what you'd want. You can have whichever."

"We could share?" The look she slants up at me from beneath a thick lock of her hair seems to say something else. Something more.

Probably my wishful thinking. This is a salad and a roast vegetable tray we're talking about, not the state of our friendship. "Sure."

"Great."

I want to stab her with a spork. Instead I wait until she's slipped a forkful of eggplant between her lips. "You once said you could make me come until I begged you to stop."

She chokes. Though she lifts a hand to delicately cover her lips, she sputters. Her eyes are wide and watery.

I spear a chickpea from the salad as if that's going to be sufficient to hide my smirk. And I wait. I wait patiently as she gathers her air and chews and finally manages to swallow.

"I was drunk."

"Does that mean it wasn't true?"

"It means it was unwise to say." Pari puts down her fork and leans back in the chair she chose, probably so that she didn't have to sit too close to me.

"You've been avoiding me."

"There's a lot to get ready for the wedding."

"Which you've been using to avoid me."

She's watching me carefully. I can see her measuring her words one by one. Taking out possibilities and rolling the feel of them between her teeth and cheeks before deciding on a combination she approves of. "It was only a couple weeks ago that, I believe, you were avoiding me. I let you have your space."

"You did." I fold the hem of my skirt over and over, until I'm not folding anymore, I'm smashing the fabric between my damp palms. "But things are different now."

"How so?"

I look up at her, and only with the full punch of Pari's gaze capturing mine do I realize that I haven't looked her in the eyes once since arriving at her office. I've lived in fear, but now I realize everything I have yet to try for. Every risk that's worth taking makes living better. "Before I knew that my life will never be the same if I don't get to taste you."

Her chest lifts and drops as if she's taken a sudden shock. Good. I want to be unmissable. I want her to be unable to pass me by.

Her lips start to part, but before she has a chance to say the careful thing she's going to, I lift a hand. Hopefully she doesn't notice that I'm shaking. It's the hand with her shining ring on it too. I want her to notice.

"I know it's not smart. It's not wise. We have two years to be married, and then all the paperwork and interviews, and maybe we'll have to stick together longer to get you actual citizenship, not just the green card, and we're just muddying the water . . . but here's the thing. I'm pretty sure that I'm me, whether or not you have sex with me. If you're going to get sick of me, it'll happen no matter what. I'll still leave wet towels on the bathroom floor and forget to wrap up the bread so that it gets stale, even if I don't get to taste your cunt."

"You shouldn't talk like that."

"Because it's crude?"

"Because I like it."

There's a hard beat in my chest, in my body. It takes me a second to realize that's the squeezing, pulling feeling of heady lust. I swallow. My hand clenches my spork before I set it down carefully.

She likes it. She likes me. I have a hard time telling the difference between my pulse and my want.

She crooks a finger toward me. I stand and come closer to her, rounding the coffee table that's piled with uneaten food. I get close enough that the hem of my sundress flirts with her knees, but we're not touching anywhere.

Slowly, oh Christ, so slowly, she uncrosses her legs and spreads them out one by one. Her expensive, decadent high heels bracket me. The carpeting is cream, making the orange leather even more vibrant by contrast.

"Up here," she says. Her voice is as lovely and lilting as ever, but there's no doubting the crispness of an order. "Look at me, not my shoes."

I have to swallow before I can crane my gaze upward. I take my time, lingering over the tender curve of her thighs, encased in snug, dark denim. The hem of her tunic is tangled on a belt that is barely sturdy enough to be called a belt. Mostly it's finely wrought wire, the better to trap a woman's gaze. But my next reward is the slope of her breasts. I wonder if she'll bare herself to me today, finally. My mouth waters at the thought.

"Come closer." She has both hands draped over the arms of the chair. She looks so cool and composed, but I can see the flutter of her pulse in her throat. I look for it on purpose, because I can't bear the idea that I'm alone out here.

Two small steps bring me up against the edge of the chair. My knees graze the inside of hers. Touch and contact. Heat pools deep in my pussy. I've felt this weight, this heaviness before, but usually only when I was fifteen minutes into playing with myself.

"Closer," she says again.

I lean down and put my hands on the chair, on each side of her shoulders, but she shakes her head. "No. Closer."

The only way to do that is to climb onto her lap. It's so ridiculous, but I'm instantly a thousand and one times more nervous. I'm way too huge for sitting on anyone.

But we're finally galloping down the road we've flirted around. If I call no-go the very first chance I have to lick her, I'll feel even more ridiculous than I will in Pari's lap.

I move slowly, giving her the chance to back us out of this. She doesn't. I end up with my ass on her thighs and my knees tucked along her hips at each side of the chair. I keep my hands on the back in order to keep my balance.

"Close enough?" I ask in my best flirty tone. My voice is just a little shaky. I'm surprised to hear that.

Her hands find my ass. There's nothing tentative about the way she grips me. Her thumbs find my hip bones and she palms me. Then she yanks me closer, so I'm falling over her. Half the space between us is gone.

She slides her grip from my ass, down the backs of my thighs. She kneads my tense muscles. "Relax. I promise you won't break me."

"You're tiny," I protest.

"If I'm tiny, you're miniscule." Her grip is steady, pulling me nearer and nearer.

All the fight goes out of me suddenly. I melt into her lap. I'm as small as a child and as content as one. I hide my face against the crook of her neck.

"Your skin is so soft," I mumble against her flesh.

"It's girl bonus."

"And your hair smells so good."

"Another girl bonus." I can kind of hear a smile in her tone, but I don't care if she laughs at me. I'll be a newbie lesbian any day if it gets her hands coasting up and down my back the way she's petting me.

I try to get even closer, wiggling so my knees push more toward the back of the seat and I can get us chest to chest. It's an improvement, but I wish I were lying flat on her, every inch of me aligned to every inch of her.

I kiss the neck beneath my mouth. I've found treasure that's just for me. She leans her head to the side to give me more room. I take my time exploring her. Pari, my gift, my kind soul, my favorite girl.

I learn that she likes attention on her neck, but that it's licks at her collarbone that make her sigh. I learn the soft valley between her breasts, and how she smells most like her in that spot. The citrus hint of expensive perfume, yes, but also earthiness that is simply her. I learn that she'll let me open my teeth on her flesh, but if I bite too hard she'll hiss and tug on my braid.

My mouth is wet when I smile up at her. I feel half-drugged, and it takes too much effort to keep my eyes open more than the barest of slits. I touch her neck, and she's damp from my efforts. Even better is when I touch her breast and her nipple is hard.

"No pain?" I tease.

"Not for me," and it's even thicker a tease. She's hinting at something we could do in the future, a taste that I'm not ready for yet.

But maybe I will be one day.

I squirm off her lap, until I'm sitting at and between her feet. I'm coiled around her like a worshipper. Her very own acolyte.

I tug at her belt, though not too firmly. I don't want to be responsible for breaking that wearable art. "Will you take this off? Please?"

She lifts her brow. Her mouth tucks into a smirk. "Just the belt?"

"And more."

"Say it." The inside of her bottom lip is dewy. The intensity of her gaze burns into me.

"Please take off your pants."

"Why?"

I swallow. I press my thighs together against the thudding beat that my pulse is using to remind me of my arousal. "So I can lick your pussy. Please."

# Sixteen

"Lick is such an easy word, isn't it?" She sounds lazy. She doesn't make me feel lazy though. I coast my hands up her thighs. The jeans are snug. The crease at the top of her leg is sharp with pressure. I scrape my nails over her. "Eat? Devour. Adore. Worship."

"You seem to think you can do a lot with that mouth."

"I haven't had any complaints before." The very opposite, though I choose not to say that. No one wants to hear how slutty their partner has been formerly. It's not polite to rub it in. "Let me show you."

"Men are easier than women."

"Do I get points for eagerness?"

"Absolutely." She slides to her feet as regally as an empress. I back up to give her space, but not too much because I don't want her to forget about me. Which is so insane. Like maybe if I back up one step too many, she'll shake free of this lust and realize she doesn't want to be here with me.

But her hands go to her belt first. She slides it all the way free and pools it on the tabletop.

When she unbuttons her pants, I can't look away. The sliding skitter of the zipper steals all the air from the room. Her panties are a rich, royal purple. They glow against her brown skin. I watch patiently as she toes off her heels, then pushes her jeans down to the floor and steps out of them. At least I think I'm being patient, because it isn't as if I'm pushing her back down to the chair with them still around her knees.

But I'm trembling. I think with how much I want her? Maybe also a little bit because I'm frightened of how big and important this feels to me, and mostly because I'm sure it doesn't feel that way to her.

She leaves her panties on when she sits back down, almost as if she doesn't want to startle me yet. She doesn't know me that well if she thinks any kind of sex can scare me off. But that's my fault. If she doesn't know where I've been, it's only because I haven't told her. Pari would be interested. She would listen. I don't want to think about that now, though.

Especially not when I can see a darker, damp circle at the center of the purple silk. I shove all thoughts of before into one of my small boxes. I can't seem to look away. I know she's watching me in turn.

She trails my braid through her fingers. "Take this out."

"I like having my hair back when I'm . . . working." I duck my chin. My mouth trails over the inside of her knee, which is soft enough that I scoot all of me forward in order to get closer to her, to get more of her. I'm squeezed between her legs. She helps by looping a foot around the back of my hips.

She takes the hair tie out anyway and in two snaps has it around her own wrist.

"Hey!"

"You can have it back when you've made me happy." She leans farther back in the chair, her hips tipping toward me.

"That's not fair. That's blackmail."

"You don't care." She combs through my braid enough to loosen the three hanks, but then leaves the rest to unweave on its own.

"You can't tell me what I do or don't care about."

"If you did, you wouldn't be dry humping my shin like a cat in heat."

Heat singes the tips of my ears. I bury my face against her thighs in embarrassment, but even I don't miss the fact that I manage to do so only inches from the pussy I so desperately want to lick.

I nuzzle closer. Then closer still. My lips are technically on her thighs, but I can smell her so thickly that I swear I can taste her on the air. It's a dense smell, a smell that makes me aware of myself and her as women. Hot and animalistic.

I sneak toward my prize, one kiss at a time, until I have silk under my mouth. I don't really know what I'm doing, but I take my time to learn it. The taste of her is sharp and sweet at the same time. I take all I can from the thin cloth, until I've rendered it practically useless.

Her pussy is fleshy, the lips thick. Her clit is unmissable, even through panties. I roll my tongue over that tight bead. I use my fingers to stretch the material even more taut, and it hits me like a thousand missed opportunities that my tongue is on Pari's cunt.

I go harder with my joy. I think Pari likes what I'm doing, because she's holding the back of my head firmly, but honestly it hardly matters. I like it. I'm enjoying myself.

I lift only far enough to pull the gusset of her ruined panties out of my way. It's lewd, the way I want her so much. Her inner lips glisten. Her other lips are swollen and ruddy. She already looks like she's been fucked hard, and all I've done is kiss her a little bit.

She's that swollen because she's needy. Because she's craving me. An answering thump of need practically punches me in the cunt, and I revel in it. I lean just right so my heel smashes up on my clit. When I go back to eating Pari, the rocking of my hips actually does something for me.

I insinuate one arm under Pari's thigh so her leg is resting on my shoulder. The tips of her toes graze over the top of my sundress. I squirm harder against my foot, wishing I'd had the courage to ask her to put her heels back on. Those heels mean control. I'm giving and she's taking.

Except that's happened before, and the difference now is in the way that I'm taking while I'm giving too. I could live on nothing but her breathy cries and the taste of her body forever. Especially when her fingers tangle deep enough in my hair that I can feel her nails on my scalp. Her hips jerk hard enough that I get both hands under her ass and tilt her pussy toward my mouth like it's my own private chalice to guzzle from.

I take my sustenance from the beauty that is her orgasm.

She cries out, loud and in a language I can't understand but that sounds like triumph to my ears. Her body lifts toward me, as if she can't bear to be away.

I keep licking. I keep drinking. The deluge waters my soul. I love the taste of her, especially when it grows stronger as she comes.

By the time it's all done, I have her girl cum all around my mouth. I fall backward into a sprawl that stings my elbows against the carpet.

I throw my sundress up around my waist. My feet are still trapped under my butt, with my knees splayed. The tendons that run down the insides of my thighs are so taut, it almost seems I could strum them. I'll like that image tomorrow. I'll take it out of my memories when I'm overwhelmed by the larger picture of what Pari and I have done, and I'll concentrate on the slender definition of my legs and how they're getting stronger. How my work has been worth it.

That's not now, however. Now is thrusting my fingers down the front of my panties and finding myself absolutely fucking soaked. I knew I was turned on, but this is completely ridiculous. I don't know how to touch myself when I'm like this. Normally I have to coax myself to arousal.

I'm not usually swimming in it.

When I rub my clit, I'm too soaked. The motions slide off me like I'm Teflon. I'm industrial. And also apparently a little hysterical with need. I'm rubbing around and around with three fingers, the way I normally like it, but I'm fucking teasing myself.

"Did you just growl?" Pari asks. She lowers herself out of the chair and kneels in front of me.

My eyes go wide. "No?"

"I don't know." She tiptoes two fingers up the inside of my ankle, but then she stops at my calf and strokes it. "I'm pretty sure I heard a growl."

I'm crawling inside my skin, but I force myself to hold still. I'm rewarded when she reaches for the hem of her tunic and strips it over her head. Her hair flings wild with the motion before swooping to lie about her shoulders and the tops of her bountiful breasts. She's wearing a dark-purple bra that matches her panties. I wonder what she'll do with the bra now that her panties are wrecked.

But really, I don't fucking care.

"Will you help me?" I sound plaintive. I hope it's not pushing into whiny territory. I swallow, trying to drag myself back on track. No one likes a whiner. Definitely not going to be a turn-on.

She crawls closer to me, her hips swaying in a way that makes me tremble. I let myself droop toward the ground in hopes that she'll cover me. When she does, my heart leaps. It's never been this easy before. This right.

"Do you need help?" She covers my hand with hers, the barrier of my wet cotton panties between us. She makes me rub myself harder. I let out a little noise. "Seems like you're doing well."

"I need more."

She slips her leg between my thighs and wedges us all together, my hands and her hands and her legs. So much force. So much pressure. So much traction. Exactly the more that I needed.

My head falls to the carpet. My neck cranes until I'm practically looking at the door behind me, but I don't fucking care in the least because I'm riding a wave of feeling that hasn't ever existed before. It's the shit I thought other people lied about when they took home random people from clubs and said everything was good, that they'd come so hard they'd seen stars. It had seemed like make-believe, like maybe what people said to make themselves feel better about their choices. I certainly told lies like that when I'd talked to Nikki about the guys I took home.

But this. This.

I am everything. I am the power. I'm a star fucker. I ride the crest of a dragon.

And Pari is pushing me every inch of the way. Between her leg and her hand and the control she has over my hand, she's the one fucking me. She has me, which means she has the power as well.

Goddamn, it's good.

I come in a way that makes me think I'm disintegrating. It starts in my chest instead of my pussy. Everything draws tight and then tighter, and I'm not sure I'm breathing. It doesn't matter because I'm going to take my air from some other universe. My pussy clenches next, then the sensation rides down my thighs and curls my toes.

Pari has her mouth against the top of my sundress. She nudges the cloth out of her way with her teeth. Her fucking teeth. This is insane. I love every minute of it. I preen under the attention of her mouth and lips and especially—oh, most especially—her teeth. I'm already coming, but the way she doesn't let up makes me go up and over again, and I hadn't known I could do that. I'd have put my Hitachi away by now.

But she takes me up again. She pushes my hand out of the way and yanks my underwear to the side. The sides bite into my hips in a balance of pain that's actually centering. She fucks me with two fingers at first, then three, and she curls within me in a way that seeks out the front wall of my channel. There she finds a spot that's linked to my soul, I think. When she rubs it, everything in me pulses, not just my pussy.

I make helpless noises. Stupid *uh-uh*s that sound kind of like they came straight out of porn, but they're real. So damn real.

She sucks my tight, hard nipple between her lips. Her tongue curls around it, swirling in a pattern of some sort, but I can't spare the attention to tell. It just all wraps together over and over again until I'm coming again. Or maybe still.

When the washes of sensation roll over me and my breath jerks back into my lungs, the tears come next. I cry. I don't want to, but I can't help it, like I've been unable to help so much of this. It's a dribble at first, sliding up into my hairline in a cold reminder that I'm so fucked up.

I'm pissed at myself when I sob. My arms and legs are tingling. Can't I have a chance to enjoy this before I freak Pari out?

Except she doesn't run. She doesn't seem freaked out. She shushes me with soothing noises. She wipes her hand on her shirt, then rubs away my tears with her thumbs and gathers me into her lap. "Are these good tears or bad tears?"

My butt is on the carpet, but she has me draped over her chest. I wrap my arms around her waist and bury my face in her breasts. At least I'm never too fucked up to tell how glorious they are. I'm not dead, it seems.

"I don't know," I say around sobs that feel like they could crack my ribs.

"Then just let it be."

"I'm not good at that."

She gives a small huff that is nearly a laugh, but then she kisses the top of my head. "I know. I know, Rachel."

I shiver. Such a simple thing, to be known. I crave it with all of me.

So how come I'm not sure she actually knows me at all? I know her. I'm certain of that. But I've been hiding the real me. The damaged me. Because who doesn't? I don't want anyone to see that ruined little girl, the things that drove me to places I don't even want to look back at.

I'm better now. That's what counts.

I can leave that other version of myself behind.

Far, far behind.

Eventually we move to the love seat. It's too small for us to lie intertwined the way I want, so Pari sits normally and I sit leaning against the armrest with my feet across her lap. We feed each other bites of the lunch I'd brought, and which is now long cold.

"I don't like the eggplant," Pari says, wrinkling her nose.

"This eggplant, or eggplant in general?" I want to know. I need to know everything about her. I'd crawl inside her and find a cozy place between her liver and her lungs if that didn't sound quite so fucking creepy.

"I'm somewhat hit and miss regarding it as a vegetable. It has to be cooked flawlessly." She scoops up tomatoes and chickpeas from the salad instead. "As a word, I'm quite anti-eggplant. Who looked at that thing and said, 'You know what this purple thing reminds me of? Chicken babies.'"

"By all rights, it's more like chicken fetuses. Chicken babies have feathers and say *cheep cheep*. We don't scramble them."

"I have a friend who has backyard chickens. She lives in Rancho Cucamonga. They lay so many eggs, she scrambles them and feeds them to the chickens a couple times a week."

I squeal and clap my hand over my mouth. "Cannibalism! That's cannibalism!"

Pari laughs at me. "But they're dumb, so does it still count?"

"Absolutely it counts." I'm trying to hide my laughter and act sincere at the same time. "In fact, your allegiance with a chicken cannibalist makes you suspect as well."

"This makes unfortunate sense." She leans closer and kisses my neck. I let my head fall to the side so she can have all the access she wants. "I do want to eat you. Terribly so."

Puns should not make me tremble. "Here?" I manage to squeak.

"I think I'd like to get you home so I can have you sprawled out on my bed."

"Bed is good. Bed sounds nice to me." I am as articulate as a monkey.

And as eager as one who's been offered a banana.

I get everything cleaned up in Pari's office while she packs up her laptop and some documents that she'll eventually have to work on. I sniff the air once I'm done. "You don't think . . ."

Pari looks up from where she's leaning over with one hand on her impressive desk. Her hips are cocked and her silk shirt is draping over her luscious breasts. "Think what?"

"That maybe it smells like sex in here? Should we air it out?"

"No way to." She cocks a thumb at the giant windows behind her and their view of the pale gray Los Angeles sky and the tops of a handful of buildings. "These are sealed for management's safety."

"Air freshener?" I suggest with a fairly lame shrug.

Pari strides toward me until she's close enough to hold me. "Rachel, it's fine. We're grown women. We're allowed to have sex."

"But not in your office." My neck is hot. "Someone else is going to figure it out."

She kisses me. Her mouth covers mine lazily, but I know what she's really about. Distracting me and shutting me up.

I'll take it. Gladly.

I lean into her and her kiss. She keeps her grip on my arms but drags me closer until our breasts are aligned. I know I don't have that much in the rack department, but the sensation of softness on softness is magical. I curl a hand around the back of her neck.

Her tongue delves between my teeth to touch mine. She flicks the tip of my tongue, then strokes it softly. When she breaks away, I'm gasping.

"What's happening at home?" I ask, though I know. I want to hear her say it again.

"I'm going to eat your pussy." So matter-of-fact. I love it.

We arrived in separate cars, so we go home separately, because there's no way I'm leaving my car in downtown LA if I can help it.

Even if the parking garage is by some miracle secure, I've got zero options for getting to West Hollywood for work tomorrow.

Pari kisses me again next to my car, though. It makes parting easier. I crank my music up and sing along with Beyoncé the whole way home. Impulsively, I stop at a florist and pick a huge armful of colorful tulips. Their red and yellow and purple heads nod at me from a cheap vase as I ride the elevator up to our floor.

I'm grinning and psychotically close to laughing to myself as I open the front door. I can't help it. My happy is bursting out of my seams.

I'm glad I don't though, because more people than I expect are in my living room.

Niharika is sitting on the couch, looking as elegant as she always does. Her blouse is deep burnt-orange silk, and her loose trousers match. The thick border of embroidery around her cuffs, collars, and the squared-off neckline is remarkable.

Across from her is seated a woman with a very strong family resemblance to Niharika and Pari. Her eyes aren't green, but they have the same size and distance from the bridge of her nose. Her mouth has a similar shape.

"Hi, Niharika," I say in my most cheery voice. I jostle the vase to my other arm so I can give Niharika a quick one-armed squeeze. She smiles at me and takes the flowers.

"What is this?" She holds them up. "What a lovely arrangement. They're for Pari?"

I scuff the toes of my Keds together. I guess they're for Pari, though I hadn't really thought of them that way. Just the way she might smile when she sees them in the middle of the dining-room table. I glance at the other woman in the room, and it doesn't help that she's not giving me the most friendly look. "Yeah. Do you think she'll like them?"

"Shouldn't you know?" The stranger asks archly. "You're going to marry her."

Niharika says something in Tamil that bounces off the other woman like a soap bubble. "Rachel, this is Aishwarya. She is Pari's auntie."

I put out my hand and we shake. She's got a grip that says she doesn't want to put her hand anywhere near my body. And she doesn't even know what I was doing earlier this afternoon. I'm glad I washed my hands before leaving Pari's office, or the guilt would eat me up.

"Pleased to meet you," I manage to say.

"Ai, why are you so *skinny*? Don't you ever eat?" She adds something in Tamil.

Lately I've come to love hearing that language. It means that Pari and her mother are talking in their happy, intimate way. I don't think I want to know what Aishwarya is saying. I step backward, but I don't have anywhere to go. My calves run into the couch.

"I don't know," I squeak. Lies. My illness is making me a liar again. I thought that part was long behind me. My stomach twists.

"Niharika, haven't you been cooking? Didn't you teach Pari to cook? Or is she one of those modern girls, the ones who think eating in restaurants is fine."

"She's not like that," Niharika answers. "She's a perfectly nice girl."

"How am I to know? When she's doing all this." She waves a hand in a perfect circle above her head to indicate the luridness of our den of iniquity, I think.

Niharika answers in Tamil. I try to sneak a couple steps to the side, but I stumble over the edge of the rug.

Aishwarya's attention snags on me. "What is your degree in again? I forget."

I don't think this woman has ever forgotten anything in her whole life. "I have a master's in film."

"Arts." She makes a noise I have no hope of recreating. "Why not an MBA?"

I decide saying *Because business would suck my soul dry since film already fucked me up enough* would probably be a poor choice. I'm startled when Niharika pats my wrist, but I'm relieved too. I don't want to feel alone. I've felt very much not alone all afternoon and for the past couple months that I've known Pari.

"She likes film," says a calm voice from behind me. Pari emerges from the kitchen, wiping her hands on a dishcloth. "Auntie, she has a very good degree."

Aishwarya's nose wrinkles, but she doesn't say anything more.

Pari's mom strokes my arm. "Rachel, why don't you go put these pretty flowers away."

I take them blindly, walking out of the room. I'd meant them for the dining room, but I'm not really paying attention to where I'm going, so somehow I end up in Pari's bedroom. The one I've been sharing with her since Niharika's arrival. It's got a different feeling now. The curtains are down and the light is dim.

I put the vase on the edge of Pari's desk, and it looks stupid. I try shuffling the blossoms into a different order, as if that will obscure the seam marking the two halves of the crudely joined glass vase.

Pari comes in while I'm still messing with them. She shuts the door behind her and leans against it. "Hey."

"Hey."

"Talk to me?"

"Is that what I'm going to have to deal with? At the wedding?"

I don't know if I want Pari to come closer. We don't really have the kind of relationship where this could be a hug-it-out type of conversation. Do we? Do I want us to? I settle for folding my arm across my chest and holding my elbow. My free hand makes it up to my mouth, where I rub my lips with my knuckles.

It was only two hours ago that Pari and I were fused at the mouth. Maybe I want her to hold me at least a little bit.

"It's possible." She looks sincerely worried. "I hadn't thought of it. I should have warned you. Aishwarya loves me. She wants the best for me."

"And how exactly are you guys related?"

She gives a wry twist of her shoulders. "She's . . . my mom's cousin."

I don't mean to laugh, but I do. It's not the happy, friendly kind, either. I shove my knuckles hard enough into my mouth that I feel the bite of my teeth. "So next week? It could be even worse?"

I am such a fucking idiot. I had ridden into this situation only thinking about how I could help Pari and there'd be no repercussions for me. Now I'm halfway to a goddamn relationship with Pari and only now thinking of complications.

Because *idiot.*

"I'll keep them away from you. I swear it. You can do as much or as little as you want." Pari steps toward me. She's still wearing those killer orange heels. I want to feel them on my back. "Shit, you don't even have to show up to the reception. I'll tell everyone you're sick."

"And have them talking crap about me before twenty-four hours are up? I don't freaking think so."

"There will be all the champagne you can drink."

"Do not underestimate me. I can drink a *lot* of champagne."

"You'll have to prove it." Her smile gentles me. Makes me feel a little more at ease, like I could breathe her calm into my lungs and let it push all the way through me.

"And cake. I expect the cake to be top-notch."

She lifts both hands in the air, palms out. "I swear it. *Amma* and I went to three different bakers for tastings."

"I don't understand how you've gotten any work done with her around."

"Let's just say I'll be relieved when she goes."

I won't be. I'm shocked to realize it. I'll be a little scared and a little sad once Niharika flies back to India. Not only will I miss her, but Pari and I will be alone. All the time to sink or swim, depending on our skills. Or—and this idea seems worse—to tread water in a miserable half state as we wait for the time to tick down so Pari can get her green card.

I rub my neck under the braid that I've redone. Pari brushes my hands away and starts doing it for me. She has a firm grip that works through the knots of tension in no time. "It's three days, right?"

"Mehndi and a couple other things the first day, on Friday. Second day is the religious ceremonies, and also the day we'll get our civil marriage done at the courthouse. Sunday afternoon is for the reception."

I chew on my bottom lip, which is probably distracting me from the nice things that Pari is doing to my neck, but it's not like I'm a font of control. "Doesn't it bother you? Doing the religious stuff with me, knowing that it's not real?"

She pauses in working my neck, faltering to a halt before soldiering on. "It's for a greater good. I'm unlikely to ever want to do it for 'real,' so I might as well do all this now, when it will make my mother so happy."

"If she said she wanted you to tightrope to the moon, you'd figure out a way to do it."

Pari groans. "That makes me sound slavishly devoted to her."

"I didn't mean that." I spin so fast that Pari's hands are left resting on my shoulders in a cuddling loop. "I meant it in a good way. You and your mom . . . You have an amazing relationship."

"She likes you, you know."

I squeeze my eyes shut as I shake my head. "No."

"She does," Pari insists. Her grip slides to my shoulders. "I promise."

"She tolerates me decently." My whole chest is tight. "I haven't even been around for more than that."

"You're nice and you're funny and you're sweet." Pari tucks a couple fingers under my chin and pushes my face up so I have to look at her. "Is it that hard to believe?"

I shrug. "I like her too."

"I see you not answering the question."

I sigh and let my head drop so we're forehead to forehead. Girls smell so good. Even after our earlier sex, Pari is sweetness and pears and coconut. I trail my fingertips in the very ends of her hair, which means that my knuckles are also brushing across the tips of her breast. It's on-accident-not-really, and I'm not stopping unless she tells me to. But of course she doesn't.

"I'm glad she likes me." I hold the rest of my judgment to myself, that she wouldn't if she knew how fake all this was.

Though it doesn't feel fake at the moment. When Pari kisses me with a smile on her lips, it feels a hell of a lot like real.

Especially when I hold her face between my hands and make the kiss go deeper. She obliges, her smile falling away and trading for the sweep of her tongue over mine. Her teeth against my bottom lip.

Our bodies draw closer together like dual stars, with all the weight of a thousand eternities behind us. I give myself over to the feelings. Who am I to doubt the stars?

Who am I to risk forever?

# chapter

# Seventeen

The next morning I wake up in Pari's arms. My face is pressed against her shoulder, and I have one hand on the breast nearest me. It's like I've found my new favorite toy and have no intention of letting go. But she's got one arm looped around my shoulders and the other on my wrist. Our legs are twined together. She's in this with me.

After sleep has fled me, but before I open my eyes, I wonder what we look like. I'd kill for a picture of us right now, all wound together and happy. My pale gold against her brown. Our hair is a study in contrasts, with her dark jet and my blonde.

Where's an intrusive drone when you really need one?

I crack a single eye open and peek up at Pari. She seems still sacked out. I'm not too surprised.

Still, I slip out of bed. I do it slowly and carefully, as if I'm a James Bond girl trying to escape the film alive. It hurts to have to do it, but I'm operating on an instinctual level. I need a break from the up and down that was yesterday.

Luckily, my emergency gym bag is still packed. It's not the one I use every day, because I don't love the way the strap cuts into my shoulder when I carry it and because it doesn't have a separate pocket I can zip my dirty workout clothes into. I'm particular.

I get dressed in the dark and slip out the door so silently that Pari never moves. But the light in the hallway is still on, and a wedge of gold lays itself across her. I pause to look. As I watch, she rolls to her side, and one hand slips across the empty sheets where I just was. Maybe she's looking for me.

I could crawl back into bed. Twist myself around her. Now I probably have that right, considering everything we've done over the past twenty-four hours. Pari would never notice I had left the bed.

Even better, maybe she would wake and I could kiss her shoulder in the way she likes. Things could proceed from there.

I shut the door behind myself. Because I'm apparently a fan of self-denial? Or self-torture, maybe, because the entire way to the gym, I'm thinking about how soft Pari's bed is and how good she smells and the way she kisses me when she's in the middle of an orgasm.

Walking into the glaring fluorescent lights of my gym gets me centered. Cindy, the countergirl, is folding towels.

"Hi, Rachel. You're here early." She's bleary-eyed still, even though she has her hair in her usual ultrahigh ponytail and her standard neon workout clothes on.

"Am I?" I guess so, because the clock above her head says two minutes past 4:30 a.m. So I lie, because that's what I do when countergirls make me feel uncomfortable, apparently. "I have an appointment in Los Feliz this morning."

She pulls a face. "Ugh. I hate driving the Five. I never leave Orange County if I can help it."

I let that go. It's not my business if she's batshit crazy. "Gotta go where the work calls."

"Yeah, totally." She smiles and we go our separate ways, pretending we're friends.

I suppose we're a certain kind of friends, kinda like Rhonda, who I wave to as I pass the mountain climber. She nods in return because she can't—or won't—let go of the handles.

I set up on the treadmill, but I don't push it too far. Just a steady 7.5 miles per hour that lets me settle into the sweet spot, where my head clears out and the world goes far away. I have music in my earbuds, but even that becomes part of the background. The world turns into a hum that I don't have to think about.

I run until I realize that the treadmills around me are starting to fill up with the prework crowd. I give up my machine to a middle-aged brunette lurking nearby.

As I stand there trying to get my air back, swiping my neck with the rough, bleach-scented gym towel, I eye up every single person in front of me. Most of them are in pretty decent shape, since this tends to be a no-frills sort of joint.

But not a single one of them looks actually *attractive* to me. Maybe that would change? If I knew them and they were nice to me. Maybe it would help if their mothers were charming and quietly supportive, reminding me gentleness still exists in this world.

I find space on the TRX apparatus and do balanced shoulder presses and assisted squats until I feel calm again. It takes a while. The trembling burn in my muscles takes longer to get lately. I hope it means I'll look good in my wedding dress.

I make my way to the office by nine thirty, clutching a Very Large Cup of Coffee, as my favorite little place calls it. I also have a box with scrambled egg whites Florentine, even though I had to stop at the cafe down the block to get those. The coffee shop has a whole-wheat breakfast burrito that I eat sometimes, but I'm trying to avoid cheese for the week before the wedding. The skim milk in my coffee is probably more dairy than I should have.

I drop all my stuff on my cluttered desk and have barely gotten two sips of the coffee before Julian appears in my doorway. He's tall and incredibly skinny. It's a good thing that he's never had any desire to be in front of the camera: it would make him look like a walking skeleton. Otherwise, he's pretty decent looking. His hair is sprinkled with white and usually just a little too long, hanging around his eyes. He looks like he could be the cousin of Antonio Banderas or something.

"I need you in the conference room."

"Good morning to you too." I plaster a smile on my face. "Yeah, I had a great weekend. Thanks for asking."

"Richard is on speakerphone."

"What the fuck? He never gets up before noon."

"It's five in London." He makes a tipping-the-bottle motion. "And it's been five o'clock somewhere longer than that."

"Shit," I mutter as I leave my desk and head for the conference room.

The table is huge—almost too big for the room. But Julian acquired it from a friend of a friend whose music studio hit the rocks. So it's not only giant, it's painted rocker red. I love it, the beast.

But even as I step into the room, I can hear Richard's voice coming from the speakerphone in the middle. He sounds tinny, and I'm not sure if it's the result of the booze or the distance to the UK or my annoyance with him.

I slide right onto the table, sitting cross-legged in the middle, next to the triangular speakerphone. "Richard?"

"Rachel?"

"Yeah, it's me. Where are you?"

"London. I told Julian." His exasperation is clear despite the slushing of his words.

"In a pub? In a hotel room?" I run my hands through my hair and tug. Hard. "You're not at Angela's house, are you?"

There's a pause that's entirely too long. I could recite an entire soliloquy in the time it takes Richard to piece his lie together. "I am, but it's not the same thing."

"That woman is poison for you." I shut down on the rest of my words. My hands ball into fists, and I scrub them against my eyes only to remember too late that I'm actually wearing mascara.

"We're being friends. Friendly. There're other people here too."

Richard and Angela are the epitome of on-again, off-again. She's had her own battles with substance abuse, but her biggest problem is her addiction to love. You'd think as an international star she'd have her fill of attention and adoration, but she never seems to get enough. She bounces mostly from man to man, but there have been rumors of coke-fueled orgies at her château in France.

So frankly the suggestion that there might be other people at her London town house is not a help. Odds are high at least one of them is a current paramour and she'd invited Rick to play the jealous fool for the group. "I'm going to send a taxi to get you."

"Rachel, no."

"Yes. And expect a call from your sponsor within the next ten minutes. If you don't answer your phone, my next call will be to a security firm we have on retainer." I'm bluffing, but he doesn't have to know that. I'll figure out someone to call. The fact that my production company is too poor to have a firm on retainer isn't going to stop me. "They'll haul you directly to The Kusnacht before you're even sober.

Or I'll let them put you on a plane back to the States, and you can go to The Dunes."

He's crying. I can hear it. I hold my breath long enough that my ears start to whine. I don't want to miss any hint of acceptance. "Rick, you need to read the latest pages. The treatment doc is done with them, and man, they sing. You're gonna shine. But you can act your ass off and no one will fucking touch you if you're not sober."

"Hollywood isn't what it used to be."

I know this. I don't know if I'm grateful for it. "You can be on top again."

"Call the taxi. Get me to The Dunes. Call Phil." Phillip is Rick's longtime assistant. I wonder where he is. He'll be beside himself that all this happened on his watch. "The Alps are cold. I don't want to be in the snow when I'm drying out."

"It's summer. I doubt there's actual snow." I make a "gimme" hand at Julian, and he gives me a tablet. It only takes a few swipes before I have a private car headed Richard's way.

"Upstate New York sounds nice." Rick sounds so weary; I want to cry with him.

"Promise me you'll tell them about Angela when you're in therapy."

"She was the love of my life." I hear an echoing knock in the background, and I wonder where he is. In a bathroom somewhere, with the door locked and his iPhone pressed to his ear? Richard is still a good-looking guy. He's gone stark white, but it works on him. "I'm not going to have another Angela."

"Your car is three minutes away. I want you to stand up and walk out of the house. Never put the phone down. Do not answer anyone who's there. Just listen to the sound of my voice."

"Okay." He scrambles around, probably standing up. "Okay, I'm listening."

And now I have to figure out what to say. Just fucking lovely. Panic sends my heart into my throat. I throw a look of terror at Julian, but he lifts his shoulders and spreads his hands wide.

I swallow. "Here's the brutal, honest truth, Rick. You will never, ever have another Angela. That's true."

He makes a noise like he's been punched in the stomach. I hear a woman's voice in the background.

"Are you listening to me?"

"Yes," he says, all the rawness of his life in one word.

"Someday, you will be incredibly thankful there's no Angela. Because you'll find someone else. Someone who's good to you, and good for you, and makes you realize that you're not a shitty person." I don't know what I'm talking about, but at the same time, I can't see anything but the memory of Pari's eyes as she rose above me last night. When she was soft with coming and making me feel just as worshipped. "You're okay. You're a good human, a really good person, Richard. You deserve to be loved by someone who loves you back."

He comes really, really close to saying no. I can feel his negativity through the silent line. A woman speaks in the background. Is Angela right there? God, it's got to be breaking his heart if she is. "Promise me?"

"I do. Everyone deserves it. You, especially, Richard. Why did you call here?"

"Because I knew you'd talk me down." His voice is rough. "Because I knew you'd help me go. Forever."

He's not talking to me. He's talking to Angela. Tears are slipping down my cheeks. "She might have loved what you guys used to have, but she doesn't love you now. Real love doesn't hurt. It only ever feels good. Richard, it feels safe."

"I can't wait to feel that."

"You will." I swallow. "You will."

"The car is here. I'm going to go."

He wants to get off the phone so he can mourn in the privacy of the closed-off car. I haven't known him long, but I know him well enough to be able to guess. Probably because it's the same thing I'd do in his situation.

"Julian has Phil on the other line. I'm booking a ticket for you right now. Staff from The Dunes will be waiting for you at JFK."

"Thanks."

"Richard?"

"Yeah?"

"Good luck. I'll buy you a coffee when you're out."

I have a couple more calls to make, but by the time I've run through them all, I think everything is in place. The next flight isn't for about three hours, which is potentially enough time for him to get in trouble at the airport lounge. But Phil thinks he can get a nurse he knows there in time. And the nurse is an ex-Marine, so bonus points for not letting Richard slip away.

Eventually I fall backward on the conference table. I throw my arms out to the sides, but the table's so big that I can't feel the edge. "Jesus, Mary, and Christ."

"Don't take the Lord's name in vain." Julian sketches a cross over himself. "It's only with His mercy that we made it through this."

Sure, if God's mercy meant me pouring my soul out for a has-been, could-be-once-again actor's emotional exorcism. "I still don't get why he'd call here. Call me."

Julian puts his big hand on my forehead and turns my face toward him. "You don't?"

He's looking at me in a way that says he's being Intent Julian.

"I'm so exhausted," I say. I look up at the ceiling and then close my eyes. "I was up late, and then my day started early, and then I went to the gym. Can't you just say it?"

"He sees a kindred spirit in you, Rachel."

"I've been out of rehab for more than three years. I don't restrict. I eat healthy." My omelet this morning had been double egg whites and double spinach. He's so full of shit.

But he kind of shrugs in a way that shows he doesn't care about whatever I'm saying. "I guess we've got a bit of a break for the next few weeks. You can double your honeymoon if you want."

"Thanks," I say weakly. Naturally I hadn't meant to take a honeymoon vacation at all when this started. But Julian was shocked when I told him so. I used the pressure of Rick's movie as a counter. Then Niharika showed up with her buckets of expectations. It was all we could do to keep her from booking us a trip to Cozumel.

Now though? Now the idea of two weeks hanging out with Pari sounds amazing.

"I'm promoting you to line producer for Richard's film."

I'm with it enough to crack open one eye. "I want a raise."

He names a figure that isn't huge, but it's enough to cut a few months off my loans. Everything comes back to those stupid loans eventually.

"You're going to end up owning this joint with me, kid."

"Owning a second-rate production company with financing more precarious than certain small nations. Be still, my heart." Except my heart actually is fluttering, and not in an *I'm so excited, I can't stand it* way. It's something else. All the stress of the last hour, maybe. I press a hand flat over my sternum, but that seems to make it worse.

"You could do worse in this town," Julian replies. He's watching me; I can feel it. I sit up and tug down the hem of my shirt. "If you feel like sticking around."

# Eighteen

The mehndi party is held at Aishwarya's house in Calabasas the day before the wedding. Nikki and I drive up together, and it takes close to three hours to get there in midmorning traffic. Nikki is slack-jawed when we pull up to the security gate and have to be checked against a guest list.

"Isn't this where Katie Holmes and Suri live?"

I shake my head as I navigate my beat-up Civic down streets designed with exactly enough curve to be casual and relaxed. Which seems like an oxymoron. "No, they're like a mile away. In the *fancier* neighborhood."

"Jesus Christ," Nikki mutters. "I'd hate to go in that one. I'm already feeling out of place."

I know what she means. The streets are lined with houses that swallow up their small tracts of land. They are all carefully European looking, with dark wood front doors and pitched roofs, as if Calabasas has ever even heard of snow.

The address we pull up to is more of the same. The front walk is outlined with delicate blossoms and hearty greenery. I wonder how much water must have cost them during last year's drought.

A valet in a gray vest is waiting for us at the curb, complete with a podium and key box. I trade my keys for a ticket, and Nikki and I grab our purses from the back seat. As quickly as a wraith, he disappears with my car. I stare after my taillights, wondering where he's taking it, but that's not really the point. A valet at a daytime house party is the point.

My toes and fingertips tingle as Nikki and I walk up the cobblestone front walk. Pari is doing okay for herself, but she's certainly not rich.

Her family? Rich.

"Just think, you're marrying into this tomorrow." Nikki bends down to sniff a flower. "These are heritage blooms, I think. They smell different than the new stuff."

I roll my eyes. "I'm not marrying this. Being a house and therefore an inanimate object aside, this is Aishwarya's house. Not even Pari's mom."

"I wonder what her house in India looks like."

I hadn't even thought about it. Somehow I'd decided that it would be incredibly comfortable, but that was probably more to do with my opinion of Niharika. And rugs. There would be lots of pretty rugs. Probably my cultural ignorance.

The last few days have been absolutely insane. Pari's family has been arriving in droves. Niharika has been quite strategic, deploying me to drive only the family members she believes will be friendly and open with me. She's chosen well so far. Everyone I've ferried to various hotel rooms has been incredibly sweet and kind. Pari's dad, Sadashiv, came in the day before. He was cool but polite.

All in all, I consider it a win so far.

I give myself a last-minute tidy up at the front door. I've worn comfy capris on Pari's advice. They're loose linen with wide legs, because maybe that would get me fewer "you're so skinny" comments from Pari's family. I'm wearing a gauzy blouse layered over a tank top for the same reason.

Nikki squeezes my arm. "It's gonna be great. You're a star."

"A star?"

"I don't know," she says with a shrug. "It was what I could think of. Do you see the size of this place? I think my mind is a little blown."

When a house girl answers the door and lets us in, things don't get better. Even the entry way is huge. I can't help but mentally compare it to the old beauty of the house Pari took me to. That estate was Hollywood grandeur in its vintage clothing. This place is a McMansion, the very worst of what's wrong with California lately.

The chandelier is crystal. The tables are topped in champagne marble. The floors are wide-planked maple that looks like it has been hand stained. On paper, it all sounds nice. In an everyday home, I don't think I'd ever be able to relax if I lived here. Thankfully that's not going to be a problem.

We follow the maid up one floor and down a hall to an entertainment room that lets me unclench my stomach a little. The scale is much more intimate, even though it's still a large space. The ceiling is lower and planked with teak, making it seem warmer.

A big screen and miniature stage fill one end of the room. Scattered here and there are low pieces of furniture like a table and a few ottomans, but mostly the floor is filled with cushy rugs and pillows. It's obvious we're going to sprawl out.

Pari jumps up from a pillow in the corner and nearly runs to me. "You made it."

I kiss her soft mouth, because I can and because I figure it would be an appropriate fiancée thing to do. I keep it quick though, because at the same time, I don't want to scandalize any of her family who're teetering on the edge of approval. "You didn't think I'd skip it for the world, did you?"

She shakes her head. A thick hank of hair slips over her shoulder. She looks lovely in a sleeveless blouse and capris. I like seeing her barefoot. She has a stain of red lip gloss on. I wonder if it transferred to me. Maybe I'll get to keep that little intimate mark of her with me.

"The last few days have been crazy. I'm not sure I'm capable of thinking at all."

"I'm pretty sure that's your mom's hope. Niharika is doing all the thinking. You just lay back and let it go."

She leans back against my hold on her elbows. A wrinkle appears between her eyebrows. "Are you feeling okay?"

"Like you said, it's been crazy." My pulse is doing weird things, a *pitter-trip-pat* rhythm. I think it's from the excitement of being in Aishwarya's house. It's as close to enemy territory as I've ever felt. I keep trying to take subtly deep breaths to abate the clenching in my chest, but it doesn't go away.

Before I have to come up with any better explanation, a new wave of arrivals demands our attention. I do my best to be charming, making myself talk even more than I might have in other circumstances. It seems like everyone is a little off their game at first. Conversation is stilted. Glances keep being traded.

Lesbian Indian wedding for the win when it comes to new experiences, it seems.

Maybe we're all on the same uneven footing.

It doesn't take long until most people warm up—a couple trays of snacks and music help. I find myself on a big red cushion next to Pari, who gets an identical seat. I want to hold her hand, but the mehndi artist doesn't give me a chance. She starts on the back of the hand, and what she's doing seems like magic.

She has a small plastic tube that reminds me of a pastry bag but is filled with dark brown batter. The pattern she draws is meticulous and intricate, full of symmetry and grace. The design starts at my wrists, and it seems like she moves quickly, but by the time I blink and look away, close to a half hour is gone.

"It's beautiful," I tell Pari, who's getting a similar treatment next to me.

"It is." She grins at me. "You are too."

I lean over and kiss her. The mehndi artist gives me a sniff of disapproval, but Niharika smiles at me and Nikki is positively beaming. "This is going to be good, isn't it?"

"Very good."

I'm not just talking about the mehndi pattern I'm being decorated with, and I don't think Pari is either.

I'm happy. So very happy. It burns in my chest and spills outward from there. I think I must be glowing with how good I feel.

It certainly seems like I must, because people keep warming to me. Pari's second cousin Chanda and I fall into a conversation about the intersection of culture and femininity in popular films. I'm drawing my examples from the US, and she's drawing her examples from Bollywood, but it doesn't matter, because we're excitedly tripping over each other to make the same points. We trade Facebook friendships by the end of the conversation so that I can look up a 1930s pre-code film and try to send it to her.

The mehndi woman has finished both the fronts and backs of my hands and moved on to the top of my feet when the dancing starts.

Niharika and Aishwarya go first. The music changes, and they take the small stage to dance in tandem. Their hands are elegant, each finger carefully placed. Aishwarya's generally dour expression has been traded out for one of pleasure. She likes what she's doing. At first the music is flutes and drums, but as they whirl, singing begins. It's high ululations that are completely foreign to me, and yet I still hear longing.

"I look for my love," Pari translates, leaning close to me. "In every river and every neighborhood."

I want to tease. I want to say "but you've found her," but my gaze catches with hers. Everyone else is watching Niharika and Aishwarya dance.

I can't say that. I don't know if she's found her love in me.

I've found mine in her.

I want to say it. Fear chokes me. It shoves a fist down my throat and clenches everything so tight that I can hardly breathe.

"Now my heart can't sleep nor stay awake," Pari breathes.

We're leaning closer and closer. I'm willing her to kiss me. I want it so badly, and if she touches me right now, I think I might catch on fire.

"Behave," scolds Jaya, a friend of Aishwarya. "There will be plenty of time for that later. Tomorrow!"

We jerk apart. Then I'm staring at Jaya a little dumbfounded. Did she just tease? About sex?

A gray-haired woman who was introduced to me as Aishwarya's mother is frowning at me from a seat in the back, but it's probably points on the side of good that she's here at all. I bet she's here for Pari. Everyone seems to be. Her family loves her with full hearts.

I want in. I want it all.

I want Pari for my own.

I just hope she wants me too.

Niharika and Aishwarya finish to resounding cheers Most of us can't applaud because of the mehndi paste on our hands, but I make sure to add my voice to the whooping. A squad of younger girls hop up next. They're obviously the next generation, younger than Pari and I even. I feel a little maternal as I look at them, and I nearly giggle with my happiness. This is all too much.

I don't know what to do with so much joy.

After the four of them dance what looks to be a more modern dance, there's a break. Trays of snacks get passed around.

A woman in a beautiful seafoam-green sari kneels next to me with a plate in her hands. "Samosa?"

The triangular pockets are deep-fried. I swallow against a mixed wave of lust and disgust. "No, thank you."

"Have one," says Nikki. She has one half-bitten already. She licks a flake of pastry off her bottom lip. "They're so good."

"They are seasoned potatoes inside. No meat," the woman trying to serve me says, as if I'm afraid of the contents being non-vegetarian.

I take one and nibble. "Delicious."

And they are. They're so light and crisp that they must have been cooked for only moments. Yet I still feel the grease coating my tongue. I wonder how many calories are in each little pocket.

I make myself take another bite while the woman in the sari watches, but the moment she's turned her back and I don't think anyone's watching, I wrap it in a napkin, being careful to only touch things with the mehndi-free bare tips of my fingers, and tuck it out of the way.

Except the moment I look up, I catch Pari's eyes. She saw it all.

I smile as if it's nothing while the back of my brain crumbles.

She won't love me if I'm sick. If I'm not well. Maybe she could love me otherwise, but she can't fall in love with me while I'm nasty and ugly on the inside.

I look away to hide my tears.

I keep looking at the dancers as if I'm fascinated, and true, they look like they're having a great time, but it gives me time to get calm. Or at least partly calm. I can feel the fried dough sitting in my stomach like a lump.

My hands look beautiful. My feet too. "So I don't touch this until morning?"

"Don't touch it at all," Niharika instructs me. "We'll take care of you."

Every fucking word is laden with more than I want it to be. Or it's not laden at all, and I'm just desperate to hear affection? I can't tell.

"The darker it stains, the more your mother-in-law loves you," Chanda says.

"The more your *husband* loves you," corrects another future in-law.

There's an awkward moment of silence, and then we all burst into laughter.

"Mother-in-law," Nikki says. She's taken to this *sitting on the floor* thing in full force: she's flat on her back with her head on a round pillow. "It must be mother-in-law."

"Come," Chanda says, popping to her feet. "Come learn a dance."

She doesn't hold her hands out to me, but rather waves me toward her. Obviously she's an expert at moving even while paste is decked out on her hands.

"I'm sure I shouldn't." I hold out my wrists. The design is so beautiful that I'll cry if it's ruined. Though it seems like I'm primed to cry at any provocation anyway.

"We'll take it slow. Nothing that will mess you up."

I glance at Pari. She's grinning. "Try it out. I think I'd pay money to see you try."

"That's a dare," I laugh.

Nikki shakes a finger. "Uh-oh. Them's fighting words. Rachel never backs down from a challenge."

"By all means." Pari waves toward the front of the room. The way she's lounging makes the most of the curve of her hip, and I want to kiss her there. And everywhere else I can get to.

I stand, and my head swims as if it's taking a few extra flips. Probably lust making blood rush elsewhere. I'm glad I'm not a guy, or I'd probably be sporting wood.

I do my best to push away thoughts of Pari naked. Chanda starts me slowly: how to stand just so with one arm above me and one cocked in front. Even the bend of my wrist matters. My elbow is tweaked to an angle that feels odd to me but looks natural on her.

I do my best to follow her. It seems like the party has gotten even more packed, though. More bodies, more eyes watching me. It's hotter in here too. I wish someone would turn up the air conditioning. The air is redolent with food scents.

She cheers me on when I get something right. It's probably pure luck, because I can't think straight. I see Pari. Her eyes are bright. I love her smile.

Chanda spins. I try to mimic her.

The world goes dark and I fall.

Nineteen

Hospital rooms are always so cold. I hate them. I know where I am before I open my eyes by the chill and aseptic smell. The first thing my gaze snaps to when I open my eyes is my hands. My feet. The mehndi looks mostly okay to me, though I bet more expert eyes might be able to pick out smudges. I would be heartbroken if the beauty were ruined by my carelessness.

A body shifts in the seat next to the bed. Pari. She nudges the industrial chair closer. Her hair is tousled, snarled around her round cheeks. I don't think I've ever seen her hair looking anything less than perfectly smooth.

I reach up to push it away from her face. My hand shakes. She flinches.

Tears flood my eyes. I blink them away. If I breathe through my nose, I don't cry. I don't know how or why, but it's a trick I learned when I was really young. "How long have we been here?"

"About an hour."

"I haven't been out the whole time." Things start coming back to me in bits and pieces. The guests screaming. The paramedics leaning over me.

I don't want to think about the rest of it.

I look down at my arm. There's a piece of adhesive over the inside of my elbow and a tube snaking away from it. I know what that is. I've been here before. "Fluids?"

"Including some potassium."

I nod. Been here. Done this. "I bet Aishwarya is having fucking kittens over this."

"She's not happy." Pari scoots even closer. "But mostly everyone's worried about you."

"Did you tell them?"

I can't exactly imagine it. Pari standing above my prostrate body with hands spread, telling everyone not to worry. That I was just an anorexic who'd relapsed and fucked up everything. Like usual.

Still, she shakes her head no. She's not crying right now, but I can tell that she was. Her eyes are red and puffy. "You don't have to do tomorrow."

"I'll be there."

"You're not well, Rachel." The tears start again. They're tracking down her face like lines of crystal. Diamonds. Glass. The kind that breaks and cuts you when you least expect it. "You have to get better."

I grab her hand. We're mehndi to mehndi. I wonder if that has any special meaning. Probably not. I'm probably grasping at straws the same way I'm desperately holding on to her. "I will. I promise. But after the wedding. Julian gave me two weeks off. I can call him and ask him for as much as I want. I'll go, I promise, Pari."

Jesus Christ, I'm bargaining. Like an addict begging to be fronted just a gram, only one gram, because of course that's exactly what I am. But this time I don't think I mean to avoid getting well. I want to be well with Pari. I don't want . . .

I don't want her to get away from me.

Because I know that she'll hate me if I let her get too much distance between us.

I shudder. My thoughts are so poisoned.

"I know I'm messed up," I manage to say.

"I can't ask this of you." Pari sounds as wrecked as I feel. Her voice shakes in time with her hand in mine. "It's been too much."

"This isn't your fault."

Her eyes are wide. The tears make her green shine. Her lips are damp with more tears. "How can I believe that? I feel like I'm killing you."

"No! I'm sorry, I'm sorry, you can't believe that. Don't." I struggle to sit up, but the stupid cord is in the way. I'd pull it out if I didn't know how much it would prove I'm not in my right senses. "Pari. I'm so sorry."

"I'm the one who should be apologizing to you."

"It doesn't work like that. I'm the only one responsible for myself." At least I've held on to that much from treatment. My personal responsibility flag is flying way high.

Pari's gaze drops from me and turns inward. I don't know how to get to her. We haven't actually had that long together. I can't help but remember what she said about not looking like I eat much, so long ago. It bites me.

Our hand holding has made a piece of the paste on the inside of my palm peel away. I drop it onto the waffle-weave blanket between us and turn my hand palm up. "Do you think it's dark enough?"

"What?"

"Does your mom love me?" I can't look up at her. I trace the air above the brown lines with a fingertip. My nails have gotten so stubby. I kept ignoring the way they were breaking off. "Is it dark enough?"

"Oh, darling."

She comes up from her chair and unlocks the crib-like side of my bed to swing it down. She sits on the edge of the mattress. I make room for her as gracefully as I can.

Pari holds my face between both her hands. I'm a hundred times more contained than I was within the safety of the gurney. I let my eyes drift shut. Her hands are rougher than normal because of the dried paste, but it doesn't matter. I'd know her touch in the darkness of a star.

"*Amma* loves you. Don't you know that?"

I shake my head a fraction. Not too much, because I don't want to push her away. "I don't think I knew what love felt like before."

I've handed her the perfect opening, and I'm practically begging her to take the burden of our beginning away from me.

But she doesn't. "Why did you say you'd marry me?"

"What?" It's my turn for confusion. "To help you."

"Is that it?"

That evening, at Krissy's apartment, Pari had been so beautiful. So self-assured and still calm while she discussed her thwarted ambitions. It didn't seem right that anything would be denied to her. She had everything. Culture and education and determination.

And there was still one more piece dangling out of her reach. But it was something that I could hand to her. "It was selfish," I admit. "I thought you were . . . dazzling. I wanted you to notice me."

"If anything was selfish, it was me saying yes. I knew that this was a situation that would upend our lives. I've been in a mess like this before. It hasn't worked out the way I thought it would. I thought we'd be mutually helping each other. Instead . . ."

I talk fast and a little too loud and run over whatever she's going to say next, because I can't stand to hear anything that hinges on pity. "Instead I fell in love with you."

"Instead we fell in love with each other."

Love is supposed to be a joyful thing. Pari is mournful. I'm terrified. It's a beast that lives inside me. It takes up everything, then gnaws on my bones. "Don't give up on me. Please."

It takes everything I have to say it, but I can't *not* say it.

"I'm not. It's my turn to promise. I love you, Rachel. I think I've loved you since very early on, when you came to dinner at my house and ate and I didn't know why you were shaking. How hard was it to eat that day?"

I shake my head so hard that tears fly. "Don't put that on that memory. I don't want to have been sick even then."

"But you were." She holds my wrists. "You're sick. But you can get better."

"Then you'll love me?"

"I love you *now*."

I collapse. I sob. I'm a wreck.

I'm a wreck in Pari's arms, and it's still okay.

She holds me the whole time. She pets my hair. Her shirt becomes wet with my tears and my snot, and she never pulls away. I burrow harder and harder into her softness, first her neck and then her breasts, and then somehow I have my whole face buried in her stomach. Her arms wrap around me and shelter me. I clutch her so hard that I think I might bruise her. I can't make myself stop.

I don't want to.

I don't have to.

She loves me even now, at my worst.

She's going to adore me when I shine.

# Epilogue

*One Year Later*

She looks so beautiful.

I shake when I see her. From all the goodness, all the rightness. My wife. I am hers and she is mine, and that's been true for longer than the Hindu ceremony we had yesterday, and it's also been true longer than signing our names in the courthouse on Friday.

It's been a long year, but it's been completely worth it.

I only walked away long enough to go to the bathroom, but it's like I'm seeing Pari all over again. Her pale-cream reception dress glows in the low lighting of the hall, but it's her brown skin I can't draw my gaze from. Every inch is so smooth and perfect.

I kiss her shoulder as I slip into the chair next to her. "Hello, my love."

"Hello, my wife."

I love her smile. "Did I miss anything?"

"Me, I hope."

The room is packed, but that doesn't matter to us. We're at a table at the head of the room, all alone. We're leaning close, our shoulders touching, and all I see is my woman.

Until Richard leans against the front of our table. "You two are the most frustrating couple ever."

I lift my eyebrows in challenge, but I refuse to lean away from Pari. I've worked too goddamned hard to be here. I went to treatment, and it almost killed me to be there so long, but she made it worth it.

Pari visited four times a week, called every day, and sent me care packages every week. But she never once let me off the hook of working for my treatment.

"Frustrating?" I echo. Because that's not what it feels like from the inside of this relationship. It feels like I'm finally somewhere I want to be. I'm tempted to say that I earned it, earned her, but I'm working on accepting that life doesn't work that way. "You better be careful. *The High Death* isn't out yet."

"It's postproduction. You can't scare me."

"I could tell the editors that I need some things recut?"

He's smug. He folds his arms over his chest. "You know it's a work of art as much as I do. It's going to make both of us."

"It might." Or it might be swallowed up by the hundreds of films released every year, and become a drop in the celluloid ocean. I'm proud of what we've done. That has to be enough.

"You're frustrating because you're so obviously in love."

"Good," Pari says, and now she sounds as smug as Richard did a moment ago. Her hand finds mine. We're wearing different mehndi patterns than we did a year ago, but that's okay. All of this is okay. "It's the point of all this."

"All this" is remarkable. With a year to plan, Niharika went wild. I finger a waxy petal on the bouquet separating us from Richard's hip. It trails all the way to the edges of our linen-draped table, and even goes to the floor.

I try not to care about the expense, especially on top of what it cost to cancel last year. I'd had to spend several sessions on it with April, my new therapist. Pari swears up and down that Niharika doesn't care, that we're all in this together and what matters is a wedding that establishes the family's pride in us as a couple. We used more hours to work on Pari's occasional tendency toward coolness. She'd put distance between us because she'd been scared of impermanence, burned by mistakes she'd made with Taneisha. Neither of us had that fear anymore.

"My present to you is the use of my yacht for a week, whenever you like." It's a very Richard-like move, to tell a person the present he'd gotten them, but he doesn't do it out of meanness. He wants a chance to see our happiness when we find out.

And he gets an eyeful. Pari gasps, and I grin. "Excellent!"

"I stuck a card in the pile," he adds, "But I wanted to tell you that everything's included. Staff as well. My chef will spoil you rotten."

Pari leans toward him. "What kind of chef is she?"

"The best," Richard replies, and I half expect him to add "duh" to the end of that, because he looks slightly offended.

"New American cuisine." I twirl a lock of her hair around my finger, and I'm acting like I'm all sorts of casual, but I'm excited that I'm excited about food. Richard's chef really is one of the best, and it's going to be really great food. Awesome. I'll have to remember to tell Pari about this later, and probably April too. But Pari's father is tapping a glass with the side of his knife, so I shoo Richard off. "But now you go away. Today is about us. I promise I'll drown you with praise later."

"I'm expecting the reviews to fulfill my needs," he says as he saunters off.

"Asshole," I say at his retreating back. But I'm grinning. Richard has become a better friend than I expected. It's been a little weird to have him introduce himself into my life, but he kicks surprising ass at trivia games.

"Shh." Pari nods toward her father, who's standing with a microphone in one hand and a glass of champagne in the other. "Toast time."

I steal a kiss because I can. She tastes like sweet cardamom.

"When my daughter told us that she was gay, I mourned."

Pari makes a gulping, squeaking noise, but Sadashiv lifts a hand and pats the air to reassure her. "No, no. Not anymore. But I have to speak with honesty when I'm up here. You are my only daughter. My shining star. When you went to America, I was so very proud of you. I wanted everything to be perfect for you. It was. It seemed to be. Until you told us that you wish romance with women. I was sad for the life I thought that you would lose."

I hold Pari's hand and squeeze it tight between the full white skirts of our reception dresses. She's shaking a little, but she's also nodding. Her beautiful eyes are full of tears.

"I have found much solace in my marriage to your mother." Sadashiv looks down at Niharika sitting next to him while the crowd applauds. "It was my fondest wish that you would find a partner who would give you such a soft place in the world through marriage—a marriage I would find for you, if we're being fully honest again."

I laugh along with everyone else even though Pari pulls a face at me. In apology, I lift our hands and kiss her knuckles, though there's accidental contact between my teeth and her skin. It's hard to kiss when you're dying of laughter.

"I'm pleased to say you have found for yourself the love that I wished for you." Sadashiv's gaze turns toward me. His eyes look fond and his smile is gentle. "Rachel is a lovely, kindhearted woman. When you first told us about her, you said that we'd be pleased with her optimism. It is true. You knew us, and you knew her as well. I know that I can speak for your mother when I say that we have come to love Rachel as if a daughter to us. And it is with that love in mind that I give you both this gift."

The envelope he holds out to us is red. I look at Pari and she nods, so I take it and peek inside. It's a check. A number with a bunch of zeroes on the end of it. My ears whine with a high-pitched buzz.

"Holy shit," I breathe.

The audience I've momentarily forgotten breaks into cackles.

"It's for your loans," Sadashiv says quietly. "So that you both can go forward in life without such a yoke around your neck."

I look at Pari again, but she's staring at her father. "Are you sure?"

Jesus Christ. We might actually take the money. My head spins. I've been making headway on the loans, even though my rehab was expensive. My insurance option through Julian's production company is kind of bottom of the barrel, so I had to shell out extra cash to go somewhere decent. I know it was worth it. The medical bills don't even seem that bad compared to my student loans, but to have that huge chunk of money no longer owed . . . I can't imagine it.

I shake my head. "Sadashiv, no. I can't take this."

He puts down the microphone and holds both of my shoulders. "If you had been my daughter, you would not have had to pay for college. We love you as a new daughter. Let us do this."

I'm crying. My makeup artist will be pissed, but there's nothing I can do about it. Pari leans into my side. When I throw my arms around Sadashiv, Pari claps and laughs through her tears. He's an inch shorter than me, but I still feel protected when he pats my shoulders.

"Thank you," I say, and then say it like five more times.

There's hugs all around and more crying, and Niharika joins us too. I'm in a family. I have a family. It's insane. It's amazing.

It's everything I ever wanted.

And it's not a prize. I haven't earned my happiness by dint of control. I didn't have to be good or exert my will. It simply is. My duty is only to accept and appreciate the universe as a whole.

I look at Pari again, and I kiss her, and it's still difficult to kiss when I'm smiling so damn big. But we manage. Our lips cling and slide. The room cheers.

I turn her away from the crowd. My back is to them all and at least somewhat obscures what we're doing. I cover our cheeks with my hands. I kiss her deep enough to lick tongue to tongue.

Happiness is shining from Pari. Rays reach out and twine around me, and I know I'm sending my own joy in her direction. We're forever in the flesh.

Forever in a kiss.

Dear Reader,

Thank you for reading Lorelie Brown's *Far From Home*!

We know your time is precious and you have many, many entertainment options, so it means a lot that you've chosen to spend your time reading. We really hope you enjoyed it.

We'd be honored if you'd consider posting a review—good or bad—on sites like **Amazon, Barnes & Noble, Kobo, Goodreads, Twitter, Facebook, Tumblr,** and your blog or website. We'd also be honored if you told your friends and family about this book. Word of mouth is a book's lifeblood!

For more information on upcoming releases, author interviews, blog tours, contests, giveaways, and more, please sign up for our weekly, spam-free newsletter and visit us around the web:

**Newsletter**: tinyurl.com/RiptideSignup
**Twitter**: twitter.com/RiptideBooks
**Facebook**: facebook.com/RiptidePublishing
**Goodreads**: tinyurl.com/RiptideOnGoodreads
**Tumblr**: riptidepublishing.tumblr.com

Thank you so much for Reading the Rainbow!

RiptidePublishing.com

# Acknowledgments

Twitter. You are my soul mates. Yes, all of you. Except the troll eggs.

In particular, I'll say:

Elisabeth, @duke_duke_goose (even if you fly south)

Suleikha Snyder, @suleikhasnyder (I follow all my popular television through your updates and I would be lost without them)

Jessica Luther, @scATX (who has taught me that women are *kicking ass* in sports journalism)

Heidi Cullinan, @HeidiCullinan (because writer's block happens, but so does the end of writer's block)

Alishia Rai, @AlishiaRai (pls tell more baby sis and baby bro stories. They are adorbs)

Victoria Dahl, @VictoriaDahl (for convincing me to use alien-skin aluminum foil)

# also by

## Lorelie Brown

After a seminomadic childhood throughout California, Lorelie Brown spent high school in Orange County before joining the US Army. After traveling the world from South Korea to Italy, she now lives north of Chicago. She writes about romantic trysts that happen in warm places because sleet is a sad, sad concept.

Lorelie has three active sons, two yappy dogs, and a cat who cusses her out for not petting him enough.

In her immense free time (hah!) Lorelie cowrites award-winning contemporary erotic romance under the name Katie Porter. You can find out more about the Vegas Top Guns and Command Force Alpha series at KatiePorterBooks.com or at @MsKatiePorter. You can also follow Lorelie on Twitter @LorelieBrown if you like knitting, makeup, and people lacking social filters.

Connect with Lorelie:
Website: loreliebrown.com
Twitter: @LorelieBrown
Facebook: facebook.com/lorelie.brown

# Enjoy more stories like
## *Far From Home*
# at RiptidePublishing.com!

*Stuck Landing*
ISBN: 978-1-62649-329-2

*The Butch and the Beautiful*
ISBN: 978-1-62649-436-7

## Earn Bonus Bucks!

Earn 1 Bonus Buck for each dollar you spend. Find out how at
RiptidePublishing.com/news/bonus-bucks.

## Win Free Ebooks for a Year!

Pre-order coming soon titles directly through our site and you'll
receive one entry into a drawing for a chance to win free books for
a year! Get the details at RiptidePublishing.com/contests.

CPSIA information can be obtained
at www.ICGtesting.com
Printed in the USA
LVOW12s1957211016
509750LV00003B/593/P